Praise for *Derailed* by Jon Ripslinger

"A page turner ... With strong male and female main characters, Derailed will appeal to both sexes."—*KLIATT*

"Ripslinger deserves a look."—*Booklist*

"An edgy, strongly written novel ... Highly recommended."
—*Will Weaver, author of* Full Service

Other Books by Jon Ripslinger

Derailed
How I Fell in Love & Learned to Shoot Free Throws
Triangle

LAst kISs

This book is dedicated to my grandchildren—all of whom make me proud:

Michael Kroening
Emily Kroening

Marie Ripslinger
Ann Ripslinger
Grace Ripslinger
Rose Ripslinger
Joy Ripslinger

Roxanne Ripslinger
Genna Ripslinger
Alexa Ripslinger
Jessica Ripslinger

Jennifer Ripslinger

Jon Ripslinger

LAst kISs

Flux
Woodbury, Minnesota

First Edition
First Printing, 2007

Book design by Steffani Sawyer
Cover art © 2007 by Jack Flash/Photodisc Red/PunchStock
Cover design by Ellen Dahl
Editing by Rhiannon Ross

Flux, an imprint of Llewellyn Publications

Library of Congress Cataloging-in-Publication Data for *Last Kiss* is on file at the Library of Congress.
ISBN 13: 978-0-7387-1072-3

This is a work of fiction. Names, characters, places, and incidents are either the product of the author's imagination or are used fictitiously, and any resemblance to actual persons, living or dead, business establishments, events, or locales is entirely coincidental.

Flux
2143 Wooddale Drive, Dept. 0-7387-1072-5
Woodbury, MN 55125-2989, U.S.A.
www.fluxnow.com

Printed in the United States of America

One

Wow! Windy looked different.

When she came flying out of the front door of her house, bounding across the lawn to my Ford pickup, I couldn't tell why for sure. Not her clothes. She was wearing what I expected for an afternoon outdoor birthday party on the Memorial Day weekend: blue T-shirt, gold shorts, white deck shoes.

Blue and gold are State Center High School colors.

I wore cutoff jeans, sneakers, and my gold polo shirt with the blue collar. We were dressed nearly alike. Like a brother and sister. Like our mom had dressed us for a party.

Not until Windy landed next to me in the pickup, slamming the door, smiling, did I understand what was up.

She was wearing makeup. Not a lot. Just enough. Delicate touches of blue eye shadow and mascara highlighted her eyes, and berry-brown lipstick gleamed on her lips. Tiny pearl earrings perched in her earlobes. Cool.

She slid the tip of her tongue around her lips. "What are you looking at, Billy?"

She'd been my best friend forever. Really, since birth. The things we usually did together like hunting, fishing, and canoeing didn't require makeup.

"What's with all the makeup?" I said.

"What do you mean *all* the makeup?"

She yanked the rearview mirror around, peered at herself, and ran her hand through her spiky black hair. She made a pouty mouth. "Don't I look okay?"

"Like a princess."

For the first time that I could remember, she was wearing nail polish, berry brown, the shade of her lips, and suddenly the scent of her perfume danced in front of my nose. Gardenia. She didn't often wear perfume.

She smoothed out her shirt and shorts. "If we're going to prove to the Witch you're finished with her, I have to look like a girl who wants to keep her man, and you have to at least pretend this afternoon I'm your girlfriend. You up for that, Billy?"

"I can handle it."

I readjusted the mirror. I slipped the Ford into gear

and headed out of town on County Y28, a hilly black-top winding through the Iowa countryside. Newly planted black-dirt fields of corn and soybeans stretched for miles on either side of the road.

It was Saturday—sunny, bright, and warm. Only four days of school left, and I'd be a graduate. Not Windy. She had a year left. She was sixteen, I was seventeen. Eighteen next month.

"You're really up for this?" Windy repeated. "Being my boyfriend for an afternoon in front of the Witch?"

"You don't have to call her a witch."

"I played on the same volleyball team with her for five years. She's a witch."

"We'll hold hands, kiss—whatever it takes. I'll prove she can't yank me around any longer."

"That's what I want to hear."

"I don't know how I got invited to her party, anyway. I don't fit in."

"*Duh!* So she can sink her claws into you again."

Lisa Wells, the Witch, lived off a lonely tree-lined gravel lane in the country named Castle Drive. Her dad was president of State Center University. Lisa told me once he craved solitude and that's why he rejected the idea of living in the house on campus provided by the university.

I braked the Ford to a stop off the lane and parked on the grass. Gleaming in the dappled sun, fifteen or twenty cars had parked ahead of me.

I climbed out and glanced at my watch. Two o'clock. The invitation had said the party started at one.

"Lots of people are here already," I said.

Windy stepped around to the front of the Ford. "Maybe she wants to tell you she's pregnant, that's why she invited you."

"She's on the pill."

"You know what they call a guy whose girl's on the pill?"

I tried to ignore that, but Windy dished out the answer with a smile: "They call him Daddy."

"Not funny."

Windy's hand was warm as it snuggled into mine. "I'm your girlfriend now, got it? Act like I am."

"Got it."

We crunched along the gravel lane for nearly a block, following it as it veered to the left, and suddenly I found myself in sight of Lisa Wells's house.

I'd never seen it in daylight.

Flanked with woods in the back and on both sides, the house was a two-story structure of wood, glass, and stone. Lots of peaks, porches, and decks, it perched on the top of a grassy hill that sloped fifty yards down to a lake. The Wells had no neighbors. The place sat aloof on the top of the hill, a symbol of Dr. Wells's position and importance at State Center University.

In back of the house, on a flat, wide expanse of lawn, kids romped, playing volleyball, badminton, and horse-shoes. Close to the side of the house stood an open-sided tent, bigger than a small barn, sheltering a dozen or more long, cafeteria-style tables and chairs. Gold and blue tablecloths draped the tables, and music blared from speakers hung from the eaves of the house.

"Wow!" Windy said. "What a layout."

I remembered seeing the inside of the house for the first time with its fireplaces, thick rugs, and lighted paintings on the walls, and I'd thought to myself, *Lisa lives in a palace!*

I'd never seen the house from this vantage point. Meetings between Lisa and me had always occurred at night in her bedroom after I'd paddled across the lake in a canoe.

The outside of the house with its shrubs, grass, woods, and lake impressed me as much as the inside.

As Windy and I strolled across the lawn, Eric Benson—Lisa's father-approved boyfriend—strode out from under the tent toward us.

"Uh-oh," Windy said. "Trouble already."

A senior like me, but a football jock and a brilliant student, Eric was this year's student body president. His father was a full professor in the Law Department at SCU. The word was Eric intended to enroll at the University of Michigan to study law and walk on as a football player. After he graduated, he intended to set up his own practice here in State Center.

"Wondered if you'd show." Eric stopped in front of me and pushed his glasses in place on his nose with his forefinger.

He was taller than me, solidly built, but not as thick and wide as me.

I kept my face blank.

He tucked his thumbs in the front pockets of his shorts. "What a great honor."

"I was invited. Same as you."

"Not wearing bibs today?"

I felt myself tense. Eric might think himself a stud, but there's no way I was going to let him push me around. He hadn't worked on a farm all his life. Hadn't wrestled with a hand-powered posthole digger five, six hours a day in the July sun. Lifting weights and playing football didn't measure up. Not in my book, anyway. No Irish in him, either. No O'Reilly.

Windy wrapped her left arm around my waist. She pulled me close and smiled up at me. "We almost didn't make it—nearly slipped our minds, didn't it, sweetheart?"

"Thought we'd drop by a minute," I said. "See what's happening."

Eric scowled at me. Leaned close. "I know *all* about you and Lisa." I smelled alcohol on his breath. That didn't surprise me. Eric liked to party.

Windy kissed me on the cheek. "That's over. He's mine now."

Eric looked surprised, and I gave a start, hardly expecting a kiss from Windy so quickly.

Eric adjusted his glasses. "Lisa's been under a lot of pressure lately, getting ready to graduate, trying to choose the right college. She lost sight of her goals and started doing some stupid things for a while." He eyed me.

"Like hanging with me? Forgetting about you?"

Windy squeezed my hand, signaling me to relax.

"But she's over that now," he said. "She realizes how stupid she was."

My lips thinned.

"So stay away from her," he said. "Stay in your place."

"My place?"

"Cows, sheep, pigs—on the farm! Away from Lisa."

My face heated up. I'm a blusher. It's the curse of being Irish—redheaded, freckled, and light-skinned.

My hands started curling into fists, and I felt Windy flinch as I crunched her knuckles before she wrenched her hand free of my grip.

"My place," I said, "is any place I want it to be."

Windy tugged on my sleeve, backing me up a step. "Let's mingle."

"You mess with Lisa again," Eric said calmly, "you're dead. After today, don't ever come back here. I'll take care of you personally."

"Recruit the rest of your football team."

Windy yanked on my arm, trying to drag me away. "Billy, I'm thirsty."

"Don't forget what I told you, farm boy."

I gritted my teeth.

Eric spun on his heels and marched toward the volleyball players.

I wanted to kill him.

"Look!" Windy said, jumping around in front of me, stomping her foot. "We're trying to prove you've broken the hold Lisa had on you. You've moved on."

"I know that."

"Why didn't you say you could care less about her? Why didn't you kiss me? You've never *ever* kissed me."

"I don't have to take any crap from Eric Benson."

"I'm trying to help you out here, Billy. At least make an effort to stay out of trouble."

We wandered over to the tent. Windy exchanged smiles, hellos, and high-fives with some of her volleyball buddies. I nodded and mumbled hello to everyone. I knew them because I'd watched a lot of Windy's games. My watching volleyball is how Lisa and I'd first met.

I knew hardly anyone else at the party, though. I didn't expect I would. Most of the kids here were university kids and/or jocks.

The thing you have to understand is the unique situation at State Center High School. The school features three cliques: university kids, whose white-collar parents teach at SCU and live in wooded subdivisions; city kids, whose blue-collar parents work mostly in the service industries supporting the university and live in the surrounding little towns; and farm kids, whose bib-and-boot parents live and work on farms. If you're a farm kid, you don't hang around much after school to play sports. Your butt's needed at home on a tractor.

Windy fit in because she was a jock. A non-jock, I'll bet I was the only farm kid here. Invited personally by Lisa Wells, the most beautiful, talented, and popular girl in school. Imagine that.

Under the tent, I dug out two Pepsis buried in ice in a Coleman cooler and handed one to Windy. I was still fuming about Eric. I rubbed my ice-wet hand across my forehead, held the cold can up to my cheek.

"You need to calm down," Windy said. "Your face is pink."

Suddenly two more of Windy's volleyball teammates descended on her, laughing, giggling, squealing, wanting to drag her away to play softball on a makeshift diamond behind the house. A ball hit into the woods was a home run. They needed one more girl.

"Billy and I just got here," Windy said, shaking her head. "We're together." She clutched my arm.

"Come on!" Mary Alice pleaded. "I've seen you hit the ball a mile in gym class. The woods isn't that far."

"Go ahead," I said.

Windy stepped up and whispered in my ear: "The Witch's got to see us together. Especially when she spots us the first time."

Barbara Templeton grabbed Windy's hand and started dragging her away. "C'mon before they find someone else."

Windy looked at me, begging me to rescue her.

I smiled. "Go. I'll be over to watch in a bit."

"You going to be all right?"

"Don't worry about me. Everything's cool."

I snapped open my Pepsi can, took a few icy swallows, and wandered out from under the tent. My eyes scanned the yard, lake, kids.

Where's Lisa? Why haven't I seen her yet?

Two

I spotted Lisa as she slammed out of the front door of the house and raced down the grassy slope to the lake, where a dozen kids splashed in the glimmering water.

She ran by without seeing me, her body tan and sleek, and my heart jumped.

At the water she stopped and looked back, like she sensed I was staring at her from fifty yards away. I was sure she saw me now.

She wore a short, white, terry cloth robe. She shrugged her shoulders and the robe dropped to the grass.

She was tall, willowy—a lithe athlete. A white bikini clung to her.

Even at that distance, the sight of her knocked me breathless. I remembered the first note she'd left in my locker back in April—April Fool's Day, in fact—and how the note had blown me away: *Let's meet, Billy. I know you probably think I'm a stuck-up snob, but I'm not. Where'd you get all that red hair? You should let it grow. And those blue eyes? Please meet me at Hollyhocks Park in Eldridge after school. Four-thirty. I think you're a person who's real.*

Someone touched me on the back of my shoulder, jolting me.

I whirled and lost sight of Lisa splashing in the lake.

"Lovely, isn't she?"

Dr. Malcolm Wells—Lisa's father, the president of State Center University—stared at me with dark eyes.

My Pepsi nearly slipped from my hand. I clutched the cold can tighter. "Hello, Dr. Wells."

"I'd like to talk to you, William."

Dr. Wells's baritone voice was smooth, resonant. He was dressed like most of the kids: a gold State Center High T-shirt, blue shorts, and sandals. And he was built. Probably spent a lot of time in the gym. A weight lifter maybe.

"Me?"

"You, William." His square jaw was tight, his eyes level with mine. I'm six foot.

I'd never spoken to Dr. Wells before, and I felt my throat tightening as I tried to say, "All right."

"In the house," he said. "Where we won't be disturbed."

———————

In Dr. Wells's study, I sat in a huge black-leather chair.

The air conditioning chilled me.

Sunshine filtered through the drawn curtains lighting the room dimly. The room smelled of lemon polish and wood. Bookcases housing hundreds of hardcover books lined the walls.

In front of me sat a mahogany desk, and behind the desk in a high-backed, maroon-leather chair studded with brass buttons sat Dr. Wells.

He drummed the carefully manicured nails of his right hand on the glass covering the desktop, the sound grating on my nerves. "Are you having a good time at the party, William?"

"Just got here, Windy and me, but, yeah, we're going to have a good time. All kinds of things to do."

"Keep young people busy, I say, and you can keep them out of trouble. We're going to trap shoot soon. Do you shoot?"

"Um…I hunt a lot; I've shot trap a few times."

"You've seen my gun collection?"

I felt a cautious smile creeping across my face.

I knew instantly what Dr. Wells was trying to do.

He wanted to trick me into admitting I'd been in his house before. The fact is Lisa'd shown me through the house the first night I'd been here—he'd been out of town. I couldn't have missed the gun collection. In a recreation room complete with bar and pool table, ten glass-doored walnut gun cabinets lined the walls. Shotguns and rifles, new and old—Browning, Ruger, Winchester, Ithica, a Parker double barrel—stood at attention in the cabinets.

I gathered my courage now and said, "What is it you want, Dr. Wells?"

The drumming stopped. Silence filled the room.

"I know you've been seeing my daughter."

"Not any longer."

"That I know is also true. I believe you've been in this house before." His voice was low. Like a purr. "I have a good idea what's been going on."

Heat rushed to my face again. I felt my Adam's apple bob.

"I can't police my daughter every second. She is sometimes a very foolish, impulsive child—it's not the first time she's made an error in judgment." Dr. Wells eased back in his chair. "I haven't announced it yet—I will this afternoon—Lisa is going to attend school right here at State Center. *My* university."

"That's not where she wants to go," I said. "She told me that. She wants to go far away from here."

Dr. Wells nodded slowly. "Lisa has unlimited potential. I have done very well with my own life, and I've worked long and hard to make sure her future will be brilliant."

His eyes narrowed as he leaned forward. Still a purr,

but now threatening, his voice lowered a notch. "You see, she's not leaving this area, and I'll not see her future jeopardized by her fooling around with you. Or with anyone else I don't approve of."

"Everybody has the right to choose their own friends."

"Don't entertain any more ideas about seeing her. Is that clear?"

Suddenly a doorknob behind me rattled, and someone straight-armed Dr. Wells's study door open. "We gonna shoot?"

I swung around in my chair. I'd never seen Rodney Wells before, but I knew the rat-faced skinny guy with shoulder-length dishwater blond hair must have been Lisa's stepbrother, home for the summer from college. She complained about him all the time.

The way Lisa explained it to me was that before he met Lisa's mom, Dr. Wells had been married to a widowed woman with a kid named Rodney. He adopted the boy. Later, Rodney's mom died in a boating accident, and this is the kid who now faced Dr. Wells and me.

A limp cigarette dangled from Rodney's mouth.

Dr. Wells's voice suddenly rolled out of his throat like thunder. "Rodney! When a door is closed, you *knock* before entering. And I've told you not to smoke in this house."

Rodney scissored his cigarette between two fingers and pulled it from his mouth. "Who's this dude?" He swaggered into the room in his black concert T-shirt and faded knee-torn jeans. "This the dude my sister's bopping?"

I flinched.

"Rodney!" Dr. Wells spit the kid's name. "This is a private conversation. Get rid of that cigarette!"

"Where do you want me to throw it, Dad? On the floor? No ashtrays around." Then he smirked, and to me he said, "I've been hearing them argue about you all day."

"Rodney—!" Dr. Wells heaved from his chair and stood, his fists clenched on his glass desktop, knuckles down. "Get out, Rodney!"

"We gonna shoot? Gimme the keys and I'll lug some guns out. Maybe I can win a few bucks."

"I'll take care of the guns."

Rodney smiled at me, his teeth small, yellow, and even. "Hang in there, stud." He poked the cigarette back into his mouth, puffed a cloud of smoke. "But don't let him catch you—he's mean."

"Rodney!" This time, Dr. Wells bellowed the kid's name.

Through another cloud of smoke, Rodney winked at me, marched out of the room, and slammed the door.

Dr. Wells was shaking.

He turned away from me, hands at his sides, clenching, unclenching. When he was threatening me, he'd kept his voice calm and cool. In the face of his stepson, he'd become rattled. Suddenly I didn't find Dr. Wells quite as fearsome as before.

His face appeared pinched. "Rodney is rather undisciplined." He moved to the curtain, pulled it back, and looked out. A patch of brilliant sunlight splashed on his desk.

"I'm going back to the party," I said.

He released the curtain and faced me. "I told Lisa not to invite you."

"She slipped the invitation into my locker at school through the door vents," I said. "I couldn't disappoint her."

"I'm in charge," he said, his voice calm again, controlled. "I'll not tolerate your presence in her life. That's my final word."

"Because I'm a farm kid?"

"She'll be socializing only with peers."

My face burned. "Ones you pick for her? Like Eric Benson? Someone with a pedigree."

"I know what your truck looks like, William—I don't want to see it parked around this estate again. I know where you live—I'll inform your parents as to what kind of young man you are."

I pivoted and stalked toward the door, leaving him behind me, stone-faced.

I hated Dr. Wells's threats. I hated being told to stay out of Lisa's life. First by her boyfriend. Then by her father.

Yet deep in my heart, I understood Dr. Wells's reasoning.

Lisa was destined for greatness. Besides being beautiful and an all-state athlete, she was a straight-A student. No way could I fit in with her plans. Her life. Not Billy O'Reilly. Farm kid.

And no doubt Rodney was right: Dr. Wells could be mean.

Stay cool, I told myself. Stay with the plan. Hang out with Windy at the party. Prove it's really over with Lisa. *Prove you're fully recovered, Billy.*

"Billy! *Pssst!*"

I was headed for the front door. I stopped dead in my tracks by the black-stone fireplace in the living room.

"Pssst—!"

My eyes wheeled round.

My head swung and lifted. My heart went *Wham!*

"Billy!"

Shivering at the top of the stairs in her wet bikini, her robe clutched in one hand, her blond hair clinging to her face, Lisa beckoned me up the stairs with frantic waves of her other hand.

I shook my head.

Dr. Wells might have come storming out of his study any second, right behind me. Rodney could have been lurking somewhere in the house. Or Eric. Someone might've wandered in from outside.

"Billy, I've got to talk to you. *Please!*"

Now Windy's words sailed through my mind: *At least make an effort to stay out of trouble.*

As if it didn't belong to me, I had no control over it, my head swiveled left, right. Down the hallway. Toward the kitchen. Then at the front door. My eyes searching all the while.

No one.

I drew a breath. My heart slamming against my rib cage, I bounded up the stairs two at a time. Smiling, Lisa held her bedroom door open for me.

Three

She eased the door closed and leaned against it.

Click!

She locked it.

I backed away from her, toward her bed. She smiled again, her lips wide, cheekbones high.

My eyes latched on to her. Hugged her. I totally loved her, though I'd never told her that; I'd been waiting for her to say she loved me first. But she never had. Not yet.

She stepped up to me and slipped her arms around my waist. I inhaled her scent from the lake and sunshine and slowly wrapped my arms around her, the full length of her bikini-clad body crushed against me.

"I was afraid you'd be a no-show," she said, and kissed me.

A voice in the back of my brain screamed: *Let go of her! Get out of here!*

I waited for my heart to slide back down my throat before I said, "What do you want?"

"We have to talk."

"What's left to say?"

"I saw you earlier. Then Rodney told me Daddy had you cornered in his study. I waited at the top of the stairs. We can't talk now. There's not enough time. But later."

"No way."

She strolled across the room to her bedroom's sliding-glass door that opened to a sun deck and steps. That's how I'd been able to slip into her room at night. Steps. Sun deck. Sliding-glass door. Six weeks of trysts. Of having sex. Fifteen times, total.

I touched the white chenille bedspread.

Lisa's entire room was done in white: carpet, walls, vanity, desk, night table, canopied bed, all with splashes of gold, blue, and pink for accent. I'd never seen the room filled with sunlight like this before, only moonlight and lamplight. The place was immaculate. Bed made. Spread taut. No clothes or other clutter on the floor. Dressing table neatly arranged.

In a way, her bedroom suddenly reminded me of Dr. Wells's study: everything in its place. Perfectly.

Muffin, her white Angora cat, lay on the bed, its eyes half-closed. I scratched the cat under the chin with my forefinger.

Lisa looked out the glass door and combed at her wet hair with her fingers. "They're still playing softball. Daddy wants to eat at three. It's quarter to now. He'll want me down there. After we eat, he wants to make a speech. Then he wants to organize a trap shoot. He'll be busy with guns, throwing the clay birds, making sure everything is safe. I'll meet you in the woods, where you always beached the canoe."

"Tell me what you have to say right now."

"Sweetie, there's not enough time. We don't want to get caught here." Still peering through the glass door, she stood on her tiptoes. "Oh, Daddy's out there now, talking to the catcher and batter, probably telling them it's nearly time to eat. Go down the stairs and out the front door. If you see anyone, tell them you were looking for the restroom."

She turned from the window, blond and beautiful, eyes blue, her tan the color of light honey.

"Are you pregnant?"

She flicked me a glance, and her lips melted into a smile. "Hurry, Billy. I have to change." She reached behind her neck and pulled at a string on her bikini top. Then she pulled the string behind her back. The bikini top fluttered to the floor.

I stood there a second, staring, my face feeling brick red, then bolted from the room.

Five minutes later I stood in the food line with Windy and clutched a paper plate, a plastic fork, and a plastic knife. I felt breathless. Encounters with Dr. Wells and Lisa—how red was my face, still?

"How'd your shirt get wet?" Windy said, and handed me a napkin. Her face glistened with sweat from playing softball in the sun. "Where were you? Did you see me hit a home run?"

The line moved forward two paces.

"I was talking to some guys," I said. "I…went into the house to the bathroom."

I wanted to look away, but before I could Windy nailed me with her chestnut brown eyes.

"Two Port-O-Potties near the edge of the woods," she said. "His and hers."

"I…didn't see them."

Windy stepped closer to me, her voice low, and jerked on my arm. "You found her, didn't you? I can practically smell her on you."

"I wasn't looking for her."

"Don't lie, Billy."

I'm sure my face looked on fire now.

The line moved two more paces.

I stood in front of the baked beans, smelling the

brown sugar and bacon in them. From farther down the table I picked up the smell of barbecued chicken and ribs. I saw coleslaw, potato salad, and corn also sitting on the serving table

"Uh-oh!" Windy suddenly nudged me in the ribs. "Here she comes now. On the prowl."

"Where?" I looked up.

"Hi, when did you guys get here?" Lisa strolled up to us and tossed us a smile.

"Hey," I said. "What's happening?"

She'd changed into white, cutoff, Calvin Klein jeans, lace around the edges of the legs; and a white, frilly, sleeveless blouse. Her blond hair swung free and silky to her shoulders. Pinned in the right side of her hair at the top of her head was a blue ribbon, a gold one on the left side.

"We've been here a while," Windy said brightly. She grabbed my hand and snuggled against my side.

"Nice party," I said. "Food smells good. I'm starved."

"There's plenty, and lots of things to do. Have a good time."

Windy stretched and kissed me again on the cheek, a loud smack. "Oh, we intend to."

Windy's kiss made me twitch. Lisa didn't seem to notice the kiss, but her eyes caught mine as she said, "See you later." She smiled, gave a little finger wave, and strolled away. *Awesome butt and legs.*

"Put your eyeballs back in your head," Windy said.

"Sorry."

Windy and I filled our plates and sat at a table under the tent. I shoveled beans into my mouth, ripped off a bite of chicken breast, scarfed it down, and then gulped cold Pepsi.

"What was that all about?" Windy said.

"What?"

"The Witch ignored the fact I kissed you. Then she looks you straight in the eye and goes, 'See you later.' What's with that?"

"Everybody says 'See you later.'"

"Why didn't you kiss me back, right there in front of her? On the lips. Hard."

"I—I didn't think of it."

"I'm trying to help you, Billy. But you don't seem to be paying attention."

Sitting at tables, most kids ate under the tent. Some sat on blankets in the grass under the sun and devoured their food. A few ate on the porch, others down by the water.

As kids finished eating, Lisa and Eric herded them under the tent, where Dr. Wells wanted to say a few words. A cool breeze puffed through the tent. Dr. Wells stood in its center. He turned slowly, spoke in his rich voice, and made eye contact with everyone he could. "Much has been written and said this year about the accomplishment of State Center High's volleyball team and coaches: a perfect season, a state championship. I would like to add my congratulations and say that I am happy that all of you could be here for this special celebration of my daughter's eighteenth birthday. If you'll permit my indulgence a moment, I would like to summarize the personal achievements of the graduating seniors of this team. These are the players who provided the maturity and leadership for this championship year." Dr. Wells heaped praise on all the girls but especially the three seniors, pointing out the school records they set serving, blocking, and spiking, and noted that all three had earned college scholarships. A major accomplishment.

Saving Lisa for last, Dr. Wells said, "My daughter, as precious to me as she is, does not need praise from me. She knows how I feel about her, how proud I am of her, how she has honored me and continues to honor me. However, let me take this occasion to announce that after much soul-searching, she has decided to attend college right here at State Center University."

Everyone whooped and cheered.

I glanced at Lisa, where she sat twenty feet away from me at a picnic table with Eric. She was twisting a straw around her finger, a faint smile on her face. A fake faint smile. Not the joyous smile of someone who had made up her mind about college.

When Dr. Wells said he wasn't going to waste any more time on speech making, more applause sounded. Kids rushed to congratulate Lisa, hugging her, shaking her hand. I lost sight of her in the crowd.

"You going to congratulate her?" Windy said.

"Do it for me."

"I should at least shake the Witch's hand."

I got up and strolled out from under the tent into the sunshine. I was full of chicken and ribs and needed to stretch. A breeze blew off the lake, cooling me.

I decided I'd talk Windy into trap shooting. She was good with a shotgun or a rifle. I'd seen her bag squirrel, quail, rabbit, pheasant, duck, turkey, and deer. She'd like shooting and would probably break more clay birds than any of the others.

Once her turn came, I could sneak into the woods to be alone with Lisa.

God, I hoped she wasn't pregnant.

Four

Rodney Wells was the first shooter.

Mounted on a four-by-four piece of plywood, the spring-loaded trap thrower sat on the ground. Fifteen or twenty kids had gathered around wanting to shoot. The others had gone back to swimming, badminton, horseshoes, and volleyball.

Dr. Wells explained to all of us—Rodney looked bored—that the gun should always be pointed up range, safety on. Don't turn around with it and wave it at someone, even if it's not loaded.

Dr. Wells cocked the thrower's arm, laid the clay bird

in place, and pulled the cord. The arm sprang forward and hurled the fluorescent-orange bird toward the woods. A Browning over and under .20 gauge already at his shoulder, Rodney sighted the bird in an instant, fired, and blew it to dust.

Holding hands, Windy and I stood fifteen feet directly behind Rodney. I watched closely as Rodney broke another bird and another and another, the pungent smell of gunpowder filling the air.

It appeared Rodney wasn't leading the birds but was firing as soon as his sights hit the target, then following through.

"Have you ever shot trap?" I asked Windy.

She shook her head.

"I have a couple of times. It's not all that tough. Not with a spring-loaded thrower. The birds fly in generally the same direction at the same speed."

"I see that."

"I'll shoot next, then you can give it a try."

"All right."

Rodney broke twenty-five birds in a row. He turned around and smiled smugly. "Next?"

"I'll shoot," I said, before anyone else could volunteer.

Rodney emptied the leather pouch belted around his waist that held his twenty-five spent shell casing. He tossed them into a cardboard box on the ground. Handing the pouch to me, he said, "Ten bucks says you can't break twenty-five."

Dr. Wells said, "Rodney, we're shooting for pleasure."

I dumped a box of twenty-five shells into the pouch and belted it around my waist. "Let's make it twenty," I told Rodney.

He smiled. "You're on."

"You said you've shot trap before?" Dr. Wells asked me.

"Couple of times."

He nodded and handed me the Browning. It was the most beautiful weapon I'd ever touched, its polished wood and oiled barrel glimmering in the sunlight.

A gold trigger and a pheasant-hunting scene engraved on the receiver added even more class. The piece probably cost a thousand dollars or more. I knew he had even more expensive ones in his gun cases.

"Beautiful gun," I said.

"That doesn't make it shoot straight," Rodney said. "Straight's up to the shooter."

"How about thirty bucks?" I said.

Rodney frowned.

I'd put him on the spot. He couldn't back down, not after he'd broken twenty-five birds and had made the first bet. Too many other kids watching.

"Thirty?" I repeated.

Rodney's eyes narrowed. "Forty."

"You're on."

Dr. Wells said, "The top barrel's improved cylinder, bottom's modified. You ready?"

I glanced around the crowd, searching for Lisa. Didn't see her. Maybe she'd already gone to the woods. I spotted Eric, though, waiting for a turn. Good. Windy could shoot next and Eric would have to wait his turn. Both would be busy.

"Ready," I said.

Turning, facing the firing range, I swung the gun to my shoulder a couple of times, getting a feel for it. Nice balance. I sighted an imaginary bird in the sky and followed it with the gun's sights. Satisfied, I cracked the gun open, inserted two shells, and snapped it closed.

"Everybody misses the first one," Rodney said.

"Pull," I said.

The bird shot out of the trap faster than I'd anticipated. I slammed the gun to my shoulder, sighted the bird and fired. My shot nicked the edge of the fluorescent-orange target—probably a single BB—splintering off a piece. The bigger chunk wobbled through the air like a wounded duck.

I blew out a breath. I'd been lucky.

Rodney sneered. "You going to count that?"

"He broke it!" Windy piped in from behind us.

"You want to go for fifty bucks?" I said.

"You won't break ten shooting like that," Rodney said. "Seventy-five."

"Enough!" Dr. Wells said.

I knew what I'd done wrong. I'd made a simple mistake that I shouldn't have. I hadn't followed through.

"Seventy-five bucks," I said.

I had maybe seventeen dollars on me. I doubted that Windy had more than ten. I didn't know how I'd pay up if I lost. I'd have to go home for more money.

"Pull," I said.

The clay bird winged out. I aimed, fired, and followed through. The bird exploded into dust.

"Way to go!" Windy yelled. Others applauded.

"That's only two," Rodney said. "Twenty-three more."

"Pull!" I said.

I aimed, fired, and dusted another bird. And another...and another...and another...until I broke twenty-five in a row.

Tight lipped, Dr. Wells said, "Fine shooting."

Windy jumped to my side. "Wow! You were great."

She kissed me on the cheek.

Smiling, I cracked the gun, pulled out the two spent shells, and handed the weapon to Windy. "Your turn. They fly a little faster than I thought. Don't forget to follow through." Unbuckling the pouch, I looked around the crowd. "Where's Rodney?"

"He left after the twenty-third bird," Windy said. "He's probably hiding."

"I'll be back in a minute." I handed the pouch to Dr. Wells.

"Billy! Aren't you going to watch me!"

"I won't be long."

Windy poked her bottom lip out. "Get your money later, Billy! Watch me! Billy—!"

Five

Heart racing, I dashed along the path through the woods to the lake, leaping the trunks of fallen trees. Last year's leaves rustled under my feet. I inhaled deeply. I loved a woodsy smell.

I glanced at my watch. Four o'clock.

I guessed it had taken me ten minutes to shoot twenty-five clay birds. Windy might take fifteen, maybe less. After five or ten minutes of missing me, she'd become suspicious. She'd go looking for me, ready to chew me out for not watching her, asking me where I'd been. I'd tell her I went looking for Rodney. Seventy-five bucks is seventy-five bucks. I wasn't going to let the skinny weasel cheat me.

A rabbit zigzagged in front of me down the path, then sneaked into the brush. Behind me, a gunshot rang out every thirty seconds, sometimes longer. That was Windy shooting. She'd do all right.

Lying to her again had been a rotten thing to do. In fact, I hated all the lying I'd been doing since I'd hooked up with Lisa Wells, especially the lying to my folks. I mean, my sneaking out of my bedroom at night to be with Lisa was like lying to them—they thought I was in bed sleeping peacefully under their roof. Sometimes in the morning at breakfast, after I'd been with Lisa, I had a hard time looking Mom and Dad in the eye. I thought surely they'd be able to peer into my brain and discover my secret. I always looked away, feeling guilty.

But I kept telling myself if I wanted to be with Lisa, lying was my only choice.

Another shot sounded behind me. I'd bet another seventy-five bucks Windy was on a streak.

Lisa stood at the edge of woods in knee-high grass. Facing the lake, she held her long blond hair back from her face in the breeze. I came up quietly behind her and tried to stifle my rapid breathing.

She must have heard me. Or sensed my presence.

She whirled and ran to me.

"I was afraid you wouldn't come," she said, breathless,

and then she pressed against me, kissing me. "I left as soon as Daddy went for the trap thrower."

I held her in my arms and explained how I'd gotten away.

"Rodney owes you seventy-five dollars?" she said.

She stepped back and looked at me.

"That was the bet. I broke twenty-five birds in a row."

"He doesn't have any money. Only what Daddy doles out to him from his trust fund. And that he drinks and gambles away. When he's home he steals everything in sight and sells it. My digital camera last week. A DVD player before that."

"How does he know about us?"

"He heard Daddy lecturing me about you today. I finally told Daddy I'd invited you. I had to so he wouldn't freak when he saw you. If you showed up." She kissed me again. "And you did."

"He gave me a lecture, too. Told me to stay out of your life. Said you were a foolish, impetuous child. You make errors in judgment. I'm evidently one of them."

She laughed. "In junior high I ran away to a girlfriend's house. I was going to live in her basement."

"You're kidding."

"Uh-uh. She was going to feed me—it was all so stupid. I was gone for a weekend. The girl's mother found me. Daddy's never forgotten the incident."

"Right now you'd like to run away to a different college, wouldn't you?"

"I'd rather die than go to college here. I won't have a life. I worked hard to get scholarship offers so I could escape."

"Remind him you've turned eighteen. You can make your own choices."

"I have, he won't listen."

"What's he know about us?"

"Nothing, I told you that."

"How about Eric? He jumped me when I first got here. Said he knew *all* about us."

"He's bluffing. He knows only what he saw, like us talking in the hallway in school. Then a couple of times he saw me smiling at you in the cafeteria. That made him suspicious. He started spying on me. He saw me drop notes through the vents in your locker. He reported to Daddy, and Daddy came down on me, and that's why I told you I couldn't see you again. I explained this before."

"I know."

"I didn't want you involved any longer, getting hurt." She kissed me on the cheek. "But I've missed you so much, Billy."

"Your dad thinks I've been in his house."

"He's gone a lot, he always thinks the worst."

"And that we've made love."

Lisa smiled. "You're so naïve, sweetie. Every father thinks his daughter is having sex with some guy, whether she is or not."

She traced her finger around my lips, snuggled close,

and kissed me once more. I wondered if she could feel my heart beating.

Suddenly I pushed back from her.

Why was I letting her torture me like this? We could never be together. Her dad would never allow it. He'd just told me so.

"The canoe's on the other side of the lake," she said. "Hidden in the brush. I paddled it over this morning and swam back. Meet me tonight. Please...one more time."

"What's the point?"

"You can't guess?"

"No."

She beamed a smile at me. "I want you to give me a birthday present, silly."

I stood there bursting with love and desire but said, "Uh-uh."

"The party will break up at six. Daddy always has everything planned to the second. Eric and I and Sally and Todd are going to a seven o'clock movie and—"

"I'm not meeting you tonight."

"Listen to me. After the movie I'm going to say I'm sick. Something I ate this afternoon. I'll make Eric take me home. I should be home by ten. That'll please Daddy. Once he knows I'm in bed, he'll go to bed and to sleep."

I grabbed her shoulders. "Are you pregnant?"

She laughed. "What a brilliant idea. That would ruin all Daddy's plans for me."

"I'm serious."

"I'm not pregnant." She kissed my throat, and her hands smoothed my back. "It's your turn to answer a question. What's with Windy? She's been all over you, holding your hand, kissing you."

Now was my chance to let Lisa know, though I loved her, I'd moved on. "We've become more than friends. A lot more."

Lisa smiled. "I don't believe it. She's too much of a tomboy. You've known her forever, she's like your sister."

"She's hot, we're closer now. Much closer."

"Does she know about us?"

"Most of it."

"If she was really your girlfriend, she'd be pissed at you, sneaking into my room at night. Us having sex."

"She's forgiven me, she's like that. Forgiving."

Lisa nearly laughed in my face. "I don't believe it! She's playing games."

"She's not."

"She doesn't like me, and she'd like nothing more than to make me think she'd stolen you away."

A red squirrel skittered across the branch of an oak tree, leaving the scene. That's what I should do, leave the scene.

I looked at my watch. Four-twenty. Windy would be out of her gourd looking for me. "I have to get back to the party."

"Daddy's still throwing trap. Hear the shots?"

"Can't help it, I've got to go."

"Billy, please meet me tonight…" A whispery plea.

I backed two more paces up the path I'd taken through the woods. Returning, Lisa could follow the path along the edge of the lake. No one would know we'd seen each other.

Tears gathered in her eyes. A sudden breeze from the lake lashed her hair around her face. She tugged her hair back. Her lips quivered. "Billy, please…! I'll be waiting."

I turned and ran, my footfalls rustling in the dry leaves.

I felt bad about ditching Lisa at the edge of the lake.

She told me once she hated her snotty, backstabbing, rich friends, all father-approved. She hated trying to appear perfect all the time—the perfect clothes, the perfect hair, the perfect face. She wanted the freedom to be herself.

I felt sorry for her.

She was a victim of her own popularity and a prisoner to her dad's demands. Tough life. And right now she probably couldn't see any way of making her life better. Not if she had to attend SCU. Her dad's university.

Halfway along the path, I stopped and looked back. The woods were too dense: I couldn't see the lake or Lisa.

Billy, please meet me tonight…one more time.

Six

After I left Lisa, I raced back to the trap shooters and searched for Windy. I thought Rodney might be there, too, and I'd collect my seventy-five bucks. No luck.

I checked out the horseshoe, badminton, and volleyball players. No Rodney. No Windy. I ambled down to the lake. No Rodney. Where was Windy?

I trudged back up the hill.

Maybe Rodney'd jumped in his car and had taken off. But what had happened to Windy?

I slipped into the house, nosed around, thinking I might find Rodney inside but didn't. I peeked into the rec room to admire the guns and the rest of the room: Indian rugs on a polished wood floor, a rack of deer antlers on a paneled wall, exposed beams overhead. Wet bar and stools. Pool table. A tawny leather couch and matching recliner.

When I turned to leave, I stood face to face with Eric.

"What are you doing?" he said, "Snooping around? Got your eye on those guns?"

"Looking for Rodney. Creep owes me seventy-five bucks."

"You'll never see the money. Rodney's a thief, a drunk, and a liar." Eric poked his glasses up his nose and stared at me. "You seen Lisa?"

He smelled of alcohol. Big time now. Had he been in the house stealing Dr. Wells's booze? Did he have some hidden somewhere else?

I said, "Lisa's your worry, man. All I want is my money."

I turned on my heels and left Eric standing alone. I wondered if he was smart enough, with booze on his breath, to stay out of Dr. Wells's path for the rest of the day.

Outside, by the badminton players, I ran into Mary Alice.

"Where have you been?" she said, all huffy. "You're in trouble. Windy's been looking for you."

"Where is she?"

Mary Alice smiled smugly. "Always knew she had the hots for you. She'd never admit it, though. You shouldn't have run off on her."

"Where'd she go?"

Mary Alice pointed toward the lane where I'd parked my pickup. "Headed that way the last time I saw her. Pissed!"

As I hurried across the lawn and down the gravel lane, I spotted Windy sitting in my truck.

When she saw me, she turned her head and stared into the woods.

I opened the door and piled in. "What are you doing?"

She looked at me. "I've got a better question. Where've you been?" Her brown eyes seemed frozen.

"Looking for Rodney."

That was partially true.

I sat motionless in the pickup, hands on the steering wheel. The vinyl seat, where the sun had hit it, scorched my back though my shirt, and the air away from the lake was hot, no breeze to cool it. "Are we leaving?" I said.

"What do you think?"

"So early?"

"No reason for us to stay any longer, is there? You've done all the damage you could."

I stifled a groan. I didn't want to go there.

I started the pickup. Cranked on the air conditioner. We powered up our windows.

"Where were you?" she said. "After I finished shooting, I couldn't find you."

"I told you, I went looking for Rodney."

"I shot twenty-three."

"Great."

She didn't seem too pissed.

I turned my truck around in the lane.

"I missed the first one," she said. "Then I hit ten or eleven in a row. I looked for you in the crowd. I shouldn't have done that. I lost concentration. Missed another one."

"Twenty-three is awesome. We both did all right. Nice party."

"You didn't find Rodney?"

"Uh-uh. Must've taken off."

"Were you looking for him in the woods?"

I eased the pickup down the gravel lane and looked straight ahead, waiting for what she'd say next. I felt sweat on my forehead.

"When I finished shooting," she said, "and couldn't find you, I went up the steps to this deck that goes around most of the second floor of the house. You can see the whole backyard from there. All around the woods. The lake. Everything. A perfect view."

She halted for a beat, giving me a chance to respond. I didn't.

"I'll bet part of that deck," she said, "is right outside Lisa's bedroom, isn't it?"

I still didn't look at her. Didn't answer, either.

"Of course it is," she said.

I stopped at the end of the lane, then pulled onto the blacktop. The cold from the air conditioner was starting to blast me in the face and it felt good.

"I saw you come running out of the woods, and Lisa

came dashing out by the lake a minute later. I'm not stupid, Billy."

I grabbed a breath. "All right. Look. I had to talk to her."

"You've been lying to me, Billy. All this time."

"She's really screwed up. Her dad's forcing her to go to school here. She wants to get away from him, but there's no way. She feels trapped."

"You said you were finished with her."

"She doesn't have anybody. Not her dad. Not Eric. Not her stupid stepbrother."

"Just you, Billy? Poor, beautiful, smart, popular, talented rich girl—all she has is *you*?"

"You don't know her like I do."

"Of course not. I've never slept with her."

That hurt. I bit my bottom lip. "It's like Lisa's dad will go crazy if he loses control of her."

"She's just like him, Billy. She was always freaked if she couldn't control everyone else on the volleyball team. As if the rest of us couldn't think for ourselves."

I eased the Ford up to sixty miles an hour. It's ten years old, blue, hardly any rust, and runs like a dream.

Windy and I were silent for a stretch. The sun was starting to dip behind the trees, casting long shadows across the blacktop.

I still wasn't looking at Windy, but suddenly I felt those brown eyes of hers drilling me.

"Lisa's got control of you, too, Billy. Ever think of that? Like her dad's got control of her."

"Not true."

"All the time we've known each other, Billy, we've never lied to each other. Or kept secrets, have we?"

"No."

"I even told you about Roger Duke and me, remember Roger?"

I nodded.

"I didn't hold back, lie, or pretend. I told you exactly how stupid I was, letting him get to me."

Roger Duke's the guy Windy lost her virginity to last year. What she did was none of my business, but I remember I was disappointed with her, and I still felt pissed at Roger, a senior who'd taken advantage of a sophomore. My best friend.

Windy said, "What did you guys do in the woods?"

"Talk." We were maybe two minutes from Windy's house in Long Grove, and I was damn glad.

"You hooked up with her, didn't you?"

I heaved out a long sigh. "No."

"That's all—you just *met* her?"

"That's it."

"You're lying to me, Billy. Always lying to me."

I licked my lips as I pulled into Long Grove, which consisted of a grain elevator, post office, tavern, park, and community center. No stop signs, no traffic lights. Two blocks of sidewalks and twelve streetlights. Population 350. No other moving vehicle on the road.

I parked in front of Windy's house and slipped the

pickup into park. She lived in a three-block neighborhood filled with old, two-story, wooden-framed houses with big front porches and steep roofs—lots of green grass, flowers, trees, and shade.

"The truth is Lisa wants to see me tonight," I said, still not looking at Windy.

"Ah! The Witch wants you to be her secret stud while her dad keeps her locked up at home."

"That's not true."

"Someone to do her whenever she feels lonely and horny."

"Not true."

"I hate liars like you, Billy."

I finally looked at Windy. Tears glittered in her eyes.

"I'm sorry," I said. "I know what we were supposed to prove this afternoon. I appreciate your help."

"It was nothing—believe me." She opened her door, slid to the edge of the seat, then turned back to look at me. "You're right, Billy. I wore too fucking much makeup...but it was for *you!*" And with that she hopped out of the pickup and slammed the door. I thought the glass might shatter.

I shrugged helplessly and eased the Ford into gear.

God, I hated hurting her.

What if she really did like me? I mean, like a boyfriend. Like Mary Alice had suggested.

That couldn't be, could it? I mean, after all this time, Windy and I had simply been friends. Buddies. Amigos. Comrades.

But why was she so pissed? Why did I feel a need to lie to her? If it was true, Windy liked me, she must think me the world's biggest total jerk.

Maybe you are, Billy.

Seven

Ten minutes after leaving Windy, I parked my pickup in the drive of my folks' farmyard. A cloud of dust lingered on the road in front of the house, where I'd spun the pickup's tires wheeling into the gravel drive.

Mom didn't like my doing that, raising dust. She said it all flew into the house, especially with the windows open in spring.

My golden retriever, Mallard, bounded off the house's front porch to meet me. I hopped out of the truck, and he nestled his cold nose into my hand. In the sunlight, his coat was nearly as red as my hair.

I scratched him behind the ears, petted his back, and thumped him on the sides as his tail swished.

"How you doing, Mallard? You should've seen Windy and me shoot clay birds. Not as much fun as ducks, though."

The dog barked, and I scratched him again.

My dad and mom, William and Eileen O'Reilly, own 240 acres of rolling, black, fertile farmland a mile north of Interstate 80, where I live. A creek meanders through the northeast corner of the land. Across the west fence line stands woods with deep ravines of mostly oak, walnut, and hickory, where Windy and I hunt squirrel, rabbit, turkey, and deer.

It's a certified Century Farm my folks own. Four generations of O'Reillys have farmed the land despite droughts, floods, the Great Depression, two world wars, and the turn of the century.

The farm is rich in history that has been preserved in diaries, family letters, photos, and news clippings. Before the Civil War, the O'Reilly barn was used to hide runaway slaves seeking freedom in the North.

Dad grows corn and soybeans. We keep a few head of cattle around and a couple of hogs to butcher for ourselves. I never get attached to the livestock anymore. It's like eating your own pet.

The land, the old farmhouse, wearing aluminum siding now—the barn, machine shed, silo—all will be mine someday.

I'm William O'Reilly Junior. Everyone calls my dad Will.

I felt proud, honored, and humbled that I'd been born into a family of the land with such a rich heritage, and it totally pissed me off that Dr. Wells thought I wasn't good enough for his daughter. That he didn't consider me one of her peers.

In the house in the living room, Dad was settled into his battered lounge chair across from the TV, his eyelids drooping. He's built like a tree trunk.

The house smelled of pan-fried chicken and mashed potatoes and gravy, Dad's favorite Saturday night supper.

Mom was shifting on the sofa like she was going to get up to fix me something to eat. "Got leftovers, Billy. And lemon meringue pie."

"Don't get up, Mom. I ate at the party. Stuffed myself."

She settled back into the sofa, where she'd been reading. Probably a historical romance. She liked that better than watching TV.

The clock chiming on the fireplace mantle stirred Dad. He scowled at it, then blinked at me over the top of his steel-rimmed reading glasses. He gave a vast yawn. "Party over already?"

"Windy and I left early."

Dad pushed himself up straight in his chair and scratched his head. His hair is as black and curly as black sheep's wool, gray sprouting only at the temples. Mom's hair is strawberry blond, almost red. She's slim and pretty.

I must have gotten my red hair from her side of the family, the Shannon side.

"Anything to do there?" Dad said.

"Lots. Volleyball. Softball. Swimming. Trap shooting."

Dad's forehead was pale white from wearing a Pioneer ball cap in the field, his cheeks tanned from the sun.

"You have a good time?" Mom said.

"Not bad. Lot of Windy's volleyball buddies there. Three of them got scholarships."

"Lot of foolishness," Dad said, "all that time spent slapping a ball around."

My folks are practical people, but the way they smile at each other sometimes and still hold hands makes me think they had lots of fun when they were kids. Maybe they still do. I don't know.

"Think Windy will get a scholarship?" Mom said.

"Maybe. I think she's good enough. Next year will tell."

"Pretty thing she's turned into," Dad said. "I'd marry her before she gets the notion to run off." Dad chuckled.

"What's so funny?" Mom said

"The thought of Hans and me being related through marriage."

"Don't worry," I said. "I'm sure Windy has other plans."

Dad and Hans, a fireman, have been best friends since they were kids. Windy and I grew up best buddies because the Meier and O'Reilly families did lots of things together, like camping, fishing, and vacationing. But I wondered if

I'd sabotaged the sixteen-year relationship Windy and I had enjoyed.

———————

At nine-thirty that night I lay in my jockey shorts on my bed in my basement bedroom. Dad and I'd built it. We'd built a bathroom in the basement for me, too. My bedroom used to be upstairs on the second floor, right across the hall from Mom and Dad's, but as I grew older it became too small, and Mom wanted the space for an office where she could manage the farm accounts.

My room in the basement is always cool, and I can be alone. Mallard sleeps on the floor. Mom won't allow him in the rest of the house, but she doesn't mind his sleeping in my basement room on a throw rug as long as he doesn't sleep on the bed.

I lay in the dark, the green numbers on my digital clock glowing. I reached down and scratched Mallard under the chin. The dog groaned deep in its throat.

I said, "It's been a long day, Mallard. Lisa's boyfriend jumped my ass, and her dad chewed me out. Lisa wants to see me one more time, and Windy's pissed at me. I made both girls cry. Maybe I should've been castrated. Like you."

The dog whined, and I smiled.

"Maybe Windy's right," I told Mallard. "Lisa wants me as her secret stud. Maybe once or twice a month she'll call me." I shook my head.

The dog sighed.

I sat up on the edge of the bed. Mallard sat up in front of me, thumping his tail, and I stroked his nose.

I hated sneaking out of the house at night. How many more times could I do that without getting caught? Or sneaking in and out of Dr. Wells's house—how many more times could I do that?

One more time, maybe?

So far I hadn't even come close to being caught, either by Dr. Wells or by my folks.

I reminded myself again that all this sneaking around was like lying to my folks, which I never did before meeting Lisa. Just white lies sometimes. I don't think they'd ever lied to me. If Mom and Dad found out how I'd deceived them, they might disown me. Throw me right off this farm. I'd never be able to face them. Facing Windy today had been tough enough. I closed my eyes in the dark and rubbed my forehead with my fingertips.

But maybe there was a chance of making something work between Lisa and me. She'd turned eighteen today. I'd already reminded her of that. Somehow I needed to convince her she could have her own life. She needed to say, "Screw you, Dad. I'm taking a hike."

Maybe I could help her find a place to live for the summer while she worked things out with her dad. Once he saw she was dead serious about having her own life, he'd back off. Let her attend a college of her choice. But then she'd disappear from my life.

Is that what I wanted?

I dragged my hand through my hair.

How could love be so complicated?

Knowing I was about to do something wrong again and deciding to do it anyway always dropped a terrible weight on my shoulders, like a wagonload of hay. But the facts were these: My telling Lisa I didn't want to be with her tonight, even if it might be for only one more time, had been a lie. What mattered was she wanted me, and I wanted her.

I'd never felt like this about anybody else. No one else had ever made my life so painful yet so delicious. Was this *really* love? Must be because I couldn't fight this sweet longing I had for Lisa, and I could make myself dizzy thinking about her.

I stood up and groped for my jeans at the foot of the bed.

Eight

Holding the canoe steady in the rippling waters of Lake Wells, I climbed into the craft. A fat moon hurled its light across the lake, glimmering off the water, and a million stars blazed in the black-velvet sky. A chorus of bullfrogs croaked along the weedy bank.

It was ten o'clock, exactly.

Earlier, from the phone in the kitchen at home, I'd called Lisa and had gotten her answering machine. After the sound of the beep, I whispered hoarsely, "It's me, Billy. I'll be there."

Out the side door of my house I crept. My folks couldn't

hear my truck start because their second-floor bedroom was on the other side of the house from the driveway. After listening to the local weather report on the radio, they go to bed every night at 9:00 PM. They always get up at 5:00 AM and listen to the grain and livestock futures report, also on the radio.

My truck was now hidden off the road in the woods by the lake.

I dipped the canoe paddle into the water first on my right and stroked, then on my left. The canoe glided effortlessly through the silent water. A hundred acres, the lake was oblong, like a football, the laces running east and west. I was paddling across the west end of the laces and would reach the opposite shore in five minutes. On the east shore, floodlights topped three telephone poles in Dr. Wells's sloping front yard.

Rodney worried me.

This was the first time I'd had to contend with his being home. Was the creep lurking in the house, drinking Dr. Wells's booze? Would he hear Lisa and me? Would he come home late drunk, smash into things, and wake Dr. Wells?

One thing about it, Lisa always locked her bedroom door with a deadbolt, for privacy she'd told me, and to keep Rodney out so he couldn't steal her things. If anyone came pounding on Lisa's door for whatever reason, I knew I could escape through the sliding-glass door, skip down the steps, then bolt across the yard and disappear into the woods.

I stroked harder. The night air smelled sweet and felt cool on my forehead and arms.

Another stroke. My heart beat faster.

My flashlight beam cut through the darkness, bobbing and jumping, and lighted the path through the woods. No matter how bright the moon and stars, the tall trees and their thick branches, even without a midsummer canopy of full-blooming leaves, blocked the light.

The dark I didn't mind—my feet knew the way—but I hated the feeling of dew-wet cobwebs smacking my face, and sometimes the sudden screech of an owl high above me chilled my blood.

At the edge of the woods I doused the flashlight and peered across the lawn toward Dr. Wells's house. The yard was alive with the sound of a thousand crickets.

I smiled. At a corner of the house on the second floor a light burned in Lisa's bedroom. She was waiting for me.

No time to waste.

I stuffed the flashlight into my back pocket and began sprinting the seventy-five yards across the grass to the side of the house, where I'd silently climb the stairs, cross the deck, then tap on the sliding-glass door to Lisa's bedroom.

But when I was twenty feet from the house, the yard suddenly lit up like a ballpark. The lights blinding me, I stopped, paralyzed—a wide-eyed deer caught in the glare of car headlights.

My heart beat at panic speed.

My head swiveled left, right.

Oh, man! Oh shit!

I knew instantly what'd happened.

I'd been caught in motion lights. They'd never been there before.

I could flee back to the woods and escape. But there'd be no meeting with Lisa tonight. Maybe not ever again.

Keeping low, I darted through the lights' glare to the house and scrambled up the deck stairs on my hands and knees. I flattened myself on the deck, just around the corner from Lisa's room.

The lights flooded the lawn from the underside of the deck. Where I lay on the deck, my heart throbbing against the wood, all was darkness.

Below me, I heard a click and the sliding of a door. I took a deep breath and held it.

"Who's out there?" It was Dr. Wells's voice penetrating the night, floating up to me. "I have a gun!"

My skin crawled.

From around the corner, I heard Lisa's door slide open. "Daddy?"

"Stay in your room," Dr. Wells called up. The command came from directly below me. Then, "Who's out there?" he demanded again.

"There's no one—" Lisa's voice.

"Stay inside, Lisa!"

"It was a deer, Daddy—two of them. I was looking out my window, watching them. Two deer."

"Deer? Are you positive?"

"I was watching them in the moonlight. Maybe those lights aren't a good idea if they're going to go on all the time."

"Go back to bed."

"Nobody's out there, Daddy. It was deer, I'm telling you. Honest! They ran away when the lights came on."

"I told you, go back to bed."

All went silent, but I knew Dr. Wells was still listening for the sound of an intruder. Even the crickets were silent, listening.

"There's no one, Daddy."

"Go back to bed."

Lisa's door slid closed, didn't click.

I hugged the deck and held my breath again.

What if Dr. Wells came up on the deck for a better view of the yard? I'd have to leap from the deck and run. Pray I didn't break a leg. Or get shot in the back.

Suddenly the lights flicked off. I heard Dr. Wells mumbling to himself, heard the glass door sliding and clicking. I remained flat on the deck, barely breathing now. I figured Dr. Wells wouldn't go straight to bed. He'd stay up and look out the window a couple of minutes before he was satisfied nobody was there.

I decided I'd wait ten minutes.

If my heart didn't explode first.

———————

Lisa slid the glass door open for me, and I stepped trembling into the darkness of her room, only the moonlight lighting my way. She'd turned out the light she'd had on earlier.

Instantly I inhaled her perfume. Lavender.

"Hey," she said almost shyly. "I knew you were out there."

She leaned into me for a kiss, but I glanced over my shoulder into the night to make sure Dr. Wells wasn't standing behind me on the deck, staring at us—her lips brushed only my cheek.

"What's the matter?" she said.

"Those lights spooked me."

"Daddy just had them installed. I forgot to tell you about them. Sorry."

"How will I get out of here without setting them off again?"

"I can turn them off from the kitchen."

I blew out a little breath. "Do you think your dad went back to bed?"

"Yes. But he's a light sleeper, I told you that before, so we have to be very quiet. I think he's edgy tonight. Where did you hide?"

"On the deck. Where's Rodney?"

"Probably stoned somewhere. He never comes home till morning."

She slid the door closed and pulled the curtain across it, cutting out the moonlight, and her face disappeared in the darkness. Coiling her arms around my neck, she kissed me.

What was she wearing? Very little. She was mostly skin.

She hugged me. Her mouth drifted across my cheek, around my neck. She felt soft and warm, and her muscles fluttered.

I held back from her next kiss.

"Don't be frightened."

I wasted no more time. "I can't do this unless we talk first."

"We'll talk later."

"Listen to me. You're not a junior high kid your dad can boss around any longer. You're eighteen years old. You can make your own choices. You can move out. Maybe that seems impossible right now—"

"It *is!*"

"But you're smart. You can find a job. Find someplace to live. Maybe your dad will change his mind. Let loose of you."

"He'd never stop ranting that I'd betrayed him—after all he'd done for me!"

"There's got to be something you can do."

"Where would I have to go to get away from him? Mars?"

"You've got to try."

"I've spent my entire life trying to please him. Not any longer…I'm not pleasing him any longer."

"What's that mean—?"

She shrugged helplessly.

"You're going to college here—isn't that *pleasing* him?"

"You don't understand…"

"Really defy him, Lisa. Piss him off. Get the hell out. Think about it—what can he do?"

"I can't…"

"Or *won't?*"

"Same thing."

I shook my head back and forth. "You're right—I don't understand."

She inched away and left me standing alone in the darkness, breathing raggedly. I heard her feet brushing across the carpet. I blinked when the touch lamp on her nightstand lit, its three bulbs lighting the room dimly through a Tiffany shade.

Whatever silky thing she'd been wearing she'd let slip to the floor. She came around the bed toward me, bathed in soft lamplight, wearing only tiny pearl earrings.

I felt all tingly and wooshy inside.

I gave in.

I let her warmth, scent, and softness overpower me.

———————

A sheet covering us, we lay in darkness on our backs in her canopied, queen-sized bed. She had tapped her bedside lamp off. A glimmer of pale moonlight fought through the curtains over the glass door, barely lighting the room.

I heard her cat Muffin purring somewhere by the bed.

The cat had always been our witness, listening to our every word, knowing our secret. A china clock ticking away on her bedside table kept time for us.

Turning toward me, she snuggled deep into my arms. "I wanted you to be here tonight so bad." She kissed my ear.

"You get everything you want?"

"Hardly ever."

"Tell your dad we belong together," I said, trying again. "We're meant for each other. Romeo and Juliet."

"Oh, Billy, Billy…" My name became a kiss. "Billy, be happy for what we've had."

I rolled over on my back and stared at the canopy.

"What do we have, Lisa? What?"

"Wonderful moments."

"Tell your dad you're eighteen. Tell him—"

"Billy, *please!* I can't."

I slammed my eyes shut. Opened them. I flapped a hand across the sheet covering us. "Tonight. *This.* Think about it, Lisa. *This!*"

"Tonight is only tonight, sweetie. Be happy with that."

"I think I love you," I said hoarsely. Swallowing. *There! I'd said it.*

She pressed a finger to my lips. "Don't," she whispered. "Don't…don't say that."

"Why not? I *love* you, Lisa." Emphatically this time.

"Don't, Billy…don't."

I broke away from her and swung my legs out of bed, my feet landing on the floor.

"*Shhhh!* We can't make any noise." She stroked my back. "Enjoy the night, Billy. One last time…please?"

I propped my elbows on my knees and buried my face in my hands. She hadn't responded with *I love you, too, Billy*—I'd given her a chance. But she hadn't said it. Not even close. My heart felt crushed, like my chest had caved in on it.

Enjoy the night…

I made love to her again, but quickly this time, without tenderness. Our lips felt dry from such fierce kissing. When it was over and I pulled back from her, I saw she was crying.

"You should go now, Billy."

I brushed her tears away with my thumb.

To argue with her again tonight was pointless.

While I fumbled for my clothes, she slipped out of bed, found the silky thing she'd worn earlier, and slid it over her arms and head, smoothed it down so that it captured the shape of her body.

When I was dressed, she said, "I'll turn the motion lights off. Give me time to get downstairs, though. Wait a minute before you leave."

I pulled back the curtain over the sliding-glass door and looked out. The moon had disappeared, only a few stars scattered across the sky. The darkness in the woods looked impenetrable.

I felt for the flashlight in my back pocket. Still there.

"Billy…I'll never forget you."

I turned and gave a start as Muffin brushed against my leg, purring.

"This is it," I said. "It's over? Last time? Forever?"

"Yes. Except for a kiss goodbye."

"You're going to hang with Eric all summer before he goes off to Michigan?"

"Eric's not good for me—I need to be away from him."

"What's that mean?"

"Just what I said."

"You're getting rid of him, too."

"I have to."

"Like you're getting rid of me?"

She kissed me again, a soft meeting of lips this time, like our first kiss in her bedroom six weeks ago. We'd come full circle.

"I'm so sorry," she said. "There's no other way."

"Right." My arms dangled helplessly at my sides.

She unlocked her bedroom door and scampered out of the room. I waited a minute, opened the sliding-glass door, stole silently across the deck, down the stairs, and fled into the chilly night.

I knew I'd lost her.

I felt it in what was left of my crushed heart.

Nine

The next morning at 8:00 AM, I was in the middle of helping Dad tear the transmission out of our old John Deere tractor. Farm machinery always seems to need repair: tractor, planter, combine, bailer. I don't know what it is, Dad likes to work on that stuff in the morning, even on Sunday, before church.

He'd dragged me out of bed at 5:30 AM.

Hands full of grease, feeling limp from lack of sleep, I stepped out of the barn a minute to grab a breath of cool morning air and to keep myself awake.

The sky was blue and cloudless, the sun rising behind

the oak tree in front of the house. Two doves cooed on the telephone line that stretched from the pole by the drive to the house.

I yawned, wiped my hands on a rag that I grabbed from the back pocket of my bibs, then rubbed my eyes with the back of my hand. After leaving Lisa, I sneaked back into my house at midnight, and when I fell into bed I couldn't sleep.

I replayed my night with her over and over in my mind, fast-forwarding, rewinding, replaying. Even this morning I was doing that. Every word, sound, touch, and scent had burned its way into my brain.

Last night, Lisa wouldn't say she loved me—I couldn't get over that. The fact kept tumbling around in my head, like clothes in a dryer. She didn't even want to hear *me* say it.

What's with that? We'd been *making* love.

I kicked at the ground with my boot.

I needed time to get over her.

I wondered how Eric would deal with his getting dumped.

I'd be glad when school was out in a few days. Lisa and I will have graduated and wouldn't see each other anymore. Two different worlds. But no one would ever convince me hers was better than mine.

Maybe…I could ask her to come out here to the farm, meet my mom and dad, see how great they are, have a huge ham or beef dinner with us. Show her how other people live. Try to convince her again she could have her own life.

Somehow I might be part of her life even if she went away to college.

Why was her old man so possessive?

I'd take her fishing. She lived on a lake, but I'll bet she'd never been fishing.

Man, all that would blow Windy away.

At my side, Mallard gnawed a huge stick, his brown eyes riveted on me.

"Drop it," I commanded.

Mallard dropped the stick and sat, his ears cocked, his eyes alert. I picked up the stick, faked throwing it twice—Mallard sat, a quivering statue—then I hurled the stick across the yard toward the front of the house.

"Fetch!" I said, and the dog exploded after his prey.

I inhaled deeply.

Nice morning.

I liked that about farming: cool, fresh mornings in the spring, but the winter mornings were cold. And sometimes, when the breeze came from the south, you could smell the stench from Mueller's hog-confinement lot five miles away. Not this morning, though. Only the earthy smell from the fields, which soon would be thriving with corn and soybeans.

Watching Mallard, I was surprised to see Windy in the family's purple Plymouth minivan speeding down the gravel road and pulling into our lane. She was definitely in a hurry.

She climbed out of the van and slammed the door.

Wearing jeans and a fluffy pink sweater, she strode toward me, obviously still pissed about yesterday. Maybe more pissed than she'd been yesterday.

Suddenly I realized the look on Windy's face wasn't her pissed look. It was a look I'd never seen on her face. Or in her eyes. Her face was blanched, like she'd just seen something horrible, unspeakable. And the expression in her brown eyes was that of total panic.

"Hey," I said, when she halted in front of me. "What's up?"

"You don't know yet, do you? You couldn't possibly know."

"Know what?"

The only thing I could think of was that maybe there'd been a big fire and something terrible had happened to her dad. Burned or something. Fell through a roof.

"My dad finished his shift this morning..." She halted.

A knot tightened in my chest. "Yes..."

"He always stops at Leo's to have breakfast with the cops coming off their shifts..."

"All right..."

"They swap stories..."

"Okay..."

"And this morning they told him..." Tears leapt to her eyes.

"Told him what?"

She swallowed, and her lips began to tremble.

"Windy, what is it? You're scaring me."

"Someone killed Lisa Wells last night."

Mallard brought back the stick and sat expectantly in front of me.

For a moment my brain seemed paralyzed, like what she'd said wouldn't register. I tried to smile—Windy must have been joking—but my face felt as if it would crack. She wouldn't joke about something like this, would she?

"Killed her?" I said. "If you're just saying that, it's not funny, Windy."

"Shot her. I'm serious."

Windy was trying to stay composed, but her lips were still trembling, and suddenly her hands were shaking. I felt almost too stunned to speak. "Shot her?"

"Her dad heard the shot in the living room. He found her on the floor."

"She's dead?" God, my brain still seemed paralyzed, unable to process the thought. My hands clenched and unclenched. My eyes filled with tears, and I swiped them away with my fingers.

Mallard growled deep in his throat, the stick clamped between his jaws.

Windy said, "There was a robbery. Someone stole some guns. They think Lisa heard whoever it was, went downstairs, and caught him in the act. He shot her and got away with four or five valuable guns."

None of it was making sense to me. I'd made love to Lisa last night…how could she be dead?

I swiped at my eyes again.

Suddenly Dad bustled out of the barn.

He looked up, surprised to see Windy, and a smile broke across his face. He tipped his Pioneer ball cap back. "What brings you around here so early, girl? I can always use another hand, especially in the morning. Come sun up this boy's about useless. Can't seem to wake up."

Windy worked her lips. Couldn't speak.

Dad hitched his thumbs in his bib suspenders. "What's wrong? You both look like you've seen a ghost. Something happen to your mom or dad, Windy?"

Windy shook her head.

"A friend of ours…" I started. But I didn't know what to say next.

Windy said, "The girl who had the party yesterday was shot." More tears pooling in her eyes, Windy repeated what she'd told me.

Dad took off his ball cap and wiped his head with a red bandana. "Who would do such a thing?"

Windy shrugged. "We were teammates. I never liked her much, but this is terrible—I'd never wish her dead. Whoever did it stole some of her father's guns."

"I can't believe it," I said.

Mallard dropped the stick and licked my hand.

"It's not in the paper this morning," Windy said. "Or on the radio yet. Probably hardly anybody knows. But there are big headlines on the sports page saying she's going to play volleyball at State Center. It doesn't say she's dead. It's so ironic."

"You said someone stole her father's guns?" Dad said.

Windy nodded.

"Kids!" he said. "One of them at that party saw them guns, liked them, and decided to come back and steal them. I'll bet on it."

Dad shuffled past Windy and me toward the house, shaking his head, Mallard following him. At the door Dad looked back. "Your mom wants to go to nine o'clock church, Billy. After eight now. Best you come in and get cleaned up."

As soon as Dad had tromped into the house, Windy turned to me and said, "The cops will probably be checking out all of the kids at the party. Sheriff Moody. You know what he's like."

I rolled my eyes. "I know."

"He'll probably want to know how well all of us knew Lisa. You should figure out what to say."

"Why? You don't think—?"

Windy shook her head. "I said Moody will probably want to know how well you know…knew Lisa. You going to tell him you were sleeping with her? She dumped you but wanted you back?"

I hadn't thought of that. "Hell, no."

"Her dad will probably tell the cops you were seeing her secretly. He knows that, doesn't he?"

"Yes."

"Eric will probably tell the cops the same thing. They're going to be suspicious. What *are* you going to tell them?"

"I don't know."

"I don't even want to know if you went to her house last night, but you better think of something, Billy." Windy bit her bottom lip. "I have to go."

I grabbed her hand. "Look…thanks for dropping by. I appreciate it."

She ripped her hand out of mine. Her chin lifted. Tears gleamed in her eyes, and her jaw turned rigid. "I'm pissed at you, Billy O'Reilly—for the rest of my life. Don't ever forget it."

Ten

"How well did you know her?" Mom said.

Mom, Dad, and I sped across the gravel road toward St. Anne's church in Dad's old four-door Chevy. Dad drove. I sat in back, the windows down, dust beginning to roll in.

In a daze, I'd dressed for church. I felt like a zombie. Unable to think. Move.

"Close the window," Dad said. "Dust's getting in."

"What?"

"The window, close it."

I rolled up the window.

"How well did you know her?" Mom said again.

"Just to talk to." I shifted, as if sitting on a thorn.

"You talk to her at the party?"

"Not much."

Once they started, how easily the lies came.

Dad glanced left and right at the miles of fenced-in black farmland. Rows of corn six inches high, planted precisely thirty inches apart, stretched over acres and acres of flat land and rolling hills.

"Going to be a good year," Dad said. "Got in the fields early. Rain at the right time. What do you think, Billy?"

"Right," I said.

But I wasn't thinking about crops. I was battering my brain with a single question: How could Lisa be dead? How could she cease to exist? *How?*

St. Anne's, an old, oak-shaded Catholic church, sits fifty yards off the road, a cemetery on one side, cornfields in back and on the other side. Last summer, volunteers, including Dad and me, painted the wooden-framed building a brilliant white. In the vestibule, an altar boy tugged on a rope, sounding the bell in the steeple—*boing! boing! boing!*—calling everyone inside for nine o'clock Mass.

Sitting in the middle of the packed church between Mom and Dad, I heard Father O'Connor's words opening the Mass, but I wasn't listening. I was thinking, thinking, thinking.

Rodney Wells.

He had to be mixed up in Lisa's death somehow.

Lisa said whenever he came home from college he stole

everything he could get his hands on. He needed money. He owed me seventy-five dollars. He probably owed others a lot more than that.

I figured it this way: Rodney fled the party after losing the bet to me. He sneaked back that night when Lisa and I were having sex, having no idea what was happening up in Lisa's room. When Lisa went downstairs to turn off the motion lights, she caught him stealing the guns. They fought. He shot her.

Mom tugged at my shirt.

Everyone in the congregation was sitting as Father began his homily, but I was still standing. Mom pulled on my shirt again, and I sat down quickly, looking around, embarrassed.

"Are you all right?" Mom said.

I nodded. Swallowed.

If I was right about Rodney's sneaking into the house to steal the guns and Lisa's interrupting him, why hadn't I heard the shot after I'd left Lisa and fled through the woods? Maybe I'd been too far away. Maybe I'd already crossed the lake and was on my way home. Why hadn't Dr. Wells, a light sleeper, awakened and stopped Rodney?

All through Mass, the mere acts of genuflecting, sitting, kneeling, standing, seemed the hardest things to do. I was just beginning to hurt, but the hurt was already so goddamned deep I could hardly breathe.

I didn't know what to say to God.

I'd been sinning but had refused to allow myself to

think about consequences. Now I'd stumbled into deep trouble and needed God's help. *I'm sorry, I'm sorry,* I told God, my head buried in my hands as I knelt, but I wondered if God was listening. I mean, since I'd ignored Him, why would *He* listen to *me* now?

After the service, I stood outside of church nodding woodenly to people I knew, mostly older people, friends of Mom and Dad.

The sun was bright and warm in the sky, but a breeze blew, promising to keep the day cool and pleasant.

Mom and Dad were talking to the Wilkersons, who farmed 320 acres south of the Interstate.

Were my parents telling them about Lisa?

Probably.

By noontime everyone in the county would know.

I decided not to stand among the groups of gossiping churchgoers. Someone else might have heard about Lisa. Someone might ask me questions about her. I wouldn't know what to say.

I looked around, then strolled across the grass toward the cemetery.

The cops weren't stupid. Somehow they'd be able to tell Lisa'd had sex before she died.

I couldn't believe she was dead.

I'd give anything to have it be a mistake. I'd go to church everyday for the rest of my life. I'd never ever make love to another girl.

Please, God!

Windy was right. The cops were going to suspect me. They'd run some kind of DNA test on me and figure out it was *I* who'd made love to Lisa. They'd think we'd fought. I must have killed her and tried to make it look as if a robber shot her.

I felt sweaty.

The grassy cemetery knoll adjacent to the church looked peaceful in the morning sunlight. Hundreds of gravestones marked the burial spots of loved ones, flowers, wreathes, and American flags decorating many stones on this Memorial Day weekend.

My folks' parents, grandparents, and great-grandparents were buried here. I came from a long heritage of honorable people. I'd never heard of anyone else in the family going to jail for robbery. Or murder. Innocent or guilty.

Was Lisa's death my fault? What if she hadn't gone downstairs to turn off the motion lights for me? Would she still be alive?

Maybe Windy's dad and the cop he'd been talking to had made a mistake. Lisa really wasn't dead. Someone else was. Someone I didn't know.

Please, God!

"Billy?"

I looked up and saw Ms. Jameison standing next to me. She was Lisa's volleyball coach. She was also my American lit teacher this semester. Lisa was taking the same course but at a period different from mine.

"You've heard, haven't you?" Ms. Jameison said, her

voice breaking. Her face was drawn and pale. Her dark eyes, red-rimmed apparently from crying, searched my face.

"About Lisa?" I said.

She nodded. "Her father called me this morning. Isn't it horrible?"

"I can't believe it. Does he know what happened?"

"He hasn't a clue—he's really broken up. As much as I dislike the way he treated Lisa, I have to feel sorry for him."

I hadn't thought about Dr. Wells's feelings, but I had to agree: this must have been a horrible experience for him, finding his daughter shot, maybe by his stepson. He must have been falling apart worse than me. I didn't like him, but I wouldn't wish Lisa's death on him. I felt sorry for him, too.

Ms. Jameison said, "He knows only that someone shot Lisa and stole some of his guns. He found her body in the living room by a fireplace." Ms. Jameison touched my arm. She was tall, dark-haired, about thirty, a former all-American volleyball player at the University of Iowa. "I know you must be hurting, too. More than anyone knows. Lisa liked you very much."

I felt my eyebrows rise. "Who told you that?"

"Lisa often confided in me. Private things sometimes. Girl talk."

"Really?"

"She had no one else. She was maybe the most popular girl in school but felt isolated. Isn't that ironic?"

"It really is. I mean, she had lots of friends, but I don't think she liked most of them."

"Her father didn't approve of you, did he? He made Lisa break off her relationship with you."

"She told you all that?"

Ms. Jameison nodded.

Head bowed, I kicked at the grass. Then I gazed up at the endless blue sky stretching over the cemetery.

I knew Ms. Jameison and Lisa had had a close relationship. It was she who had helped Lisa make scholarship contacts at universities like South Carolina, Arizona, and Stanford. Far from here. But I had no idea Lisa had told her coach secret stuff, about us, about Lisa and me.

I looked at Ms. Jameison and said, "It's Dr. Wells's fault we had to sneak around. I hated that."

"He demanded conformity from Lisa. I wanted so badly for her to break free. Now this." Ms. Jameison shrugged helplessly. "Lisa never had a chance to be her own person."

Suddenly Ms. Jameison threw her arms around me, and we hugged. After a moment, she stepped back and wiped her eyes with a wad of tissue from her purse. "Besides the emotional abuse, I think he sometimes abused her physically."

I wasn't surprised to hear that. But I said, "You think so?"

"I was never sure. But I thought a few times she came to school with bruises she didn't get from volleyball. Once with a black eye. I asked her about it, but she said she got hit in the eye with the ball in a pickup game—a guy spiked the ball at her."

"She told me she ran away from home when she was in junior high for a weekend. I'll bet she got wailed on for that."

"It's so strange," Ms. Jameison said. "Lisa came to talk to me Friday. We spent an hour at my place, but she didn't tell me her father was forcing her to go to State—she must have known."

"I didn't know until yesterday."

"I think she didn't tell me because it's the last place in the world I wanted her to go."

"I was at her birthday party yesterday and reminded her that she was eighteen, she could make her own choices."

"But I think her whole life she went where her father pointed her." Ms. Jameison dabbed at her eyes again with the wad of tissue. "What's so strange is she gave me her MVP trophy from the state tournament. Insisted I take it."

"That's weird."

"She said I deserved it more than she did because I'd put up with her tantrums for the past four years—she started as a freshman."

I gazed at the tombstones in front of me, all of them bright in the sunshine, slivers of mica in the granite stones glittering.

I still couldn't believe Lisa was dead. She'd soon be buried in the ground. None of her after-high-school dreams coming true. How unfair was that?

"I saw lots of her games," I said. "She did blow her cool sometimes."

"Still, she was a wonderful girl. No one knew how fragile. I can't believe she's gone."

"Me either," I said, and saw Mom and Dad heading for the car. "I have to go. My parents are leaving."

"I don't know any details about her death. Call me if you hear anything."

"All right."

"Kids often know more about what's going on than teachers."

On the way home, Dad turned on the radio to catch the ten o'clock news, weather, and ag report. The newscaster led off with the morning's top story: "Lisa Wells, the eighteen-year-old daughter of State Center University President Dr. Malcolm Wells, was fatally shot early this morning when she apparently interrupted a robbery at her father's lakeside home. The assailant shot Ms. Wells at close range with a small-caliber handgun and stole several valuable shotguns and rifles from Dr. Wells's collection. Police are investigating and promise a quick arrest."

"That poor girl," Mom said.

"I don't understand young people these days," Dad said.

I slumped back, my shoulders sagging.

How terrible for Lisa.

What did she think when whoever it was pointed the gun at her? How scared she must have been. Did she beg for mercy? Was she defiant?

I still couldn't believe she was dead.

Guilt washed over me. If she hadn't gone downstairs to turn off the motion lights, she wouldn't have interrupted a robbery. She'd still be alive.

With both hands I rubbed the back of my neck, trying to release the tension I felt.

Lisa's death was my fault, but I didn't kill her. Rodney killed her. Rodney is the only guy who could have gotten in without breaking in and waking Dr. Wells up. Obviously Rodney had a key—he lived there.

I puffed out a breath.

I hoped by this time the cops had cuffed Rodney and had pumped the truth out of him.

Suddenly, as Dad headed the car down the gravel road to our farmhouse, I sat up straight and stared out the window. My heart stopped, and I froze. Next to the house, gleaming in the sun in the driveway, crouched two blue and white sheriff cruisers.

Eleven

"Morning, Will." Cedar County Sheriff Henry Moody, a rugged-looking man in his tan uniform—gun, handcuffs, mace, walkie-talkie, and flashlight belted to his waist— strolled up to Dad's car, thin-lipped. "Been a long time."

Mallard followed the sheriff, barking at his heels.

Dad opened his door and slid out from behind the wheel. "Morning, Henry."

As I slipped out and closed my door, my mouth turned dry as stone.

Dad and Moody exchanged a brief handshake, one pump. Neither man smiled.

Two officers eased themselves out of the other cruiser and stood alongside it like sentries. Grim. Mom sidled around the back of Dad's car to stand by me.

"Chain the dog, Billy," Dad said.

I called Mallard to the back of the house, where I chained him to his dog house.

When I came back, Moody was saying, "Nice place you got, Will." He surveyed the house, barns, and fields. "I ain't drove by in awhile."

"What brings you here, Henry?"

The sheriff's dark eyes turned from Dad, then to Mom, appraising her. "Hello, Eileen. Been a long time, hasn't it?" He stroked his thin mustache with his thumb and forefinger.

"Hello, Henry," Mom said, lowering her eyes.

"You're looking mighty fine, Eileen."

Mom's cheeks flushed. She blushes like I do.

Dad said, "What do you want, Henry?"

"Need to talk to Billy here." Moody smiled. "How you doing, Billy?"

My throat tightened, and I tried to swallow through it. "Fine," I said hoarsely, instantly feeling the crimson heat in my face.

I'd never spoken to Moody before. I knew the cop only by reputation. He was an intimidator who bragged onstage at the high school's first assembly every year when he gave anti-drug/gang presentations that he had arrested twice as many kids in his county for speeding, doing drugs, and

drunk driving as any other sheriff in the surrounding coun-
ties. No meth labs in his county, either. Not only that, teen
violence—a national epidemic, what with school shootings
and all—was nonexistent in area schools.

Moody's gaze swept over me. "Looks like you've grown
into a real man, Billy."

I shifted my feet.

I didn't know what to say. I wasn't going to acknowl-
edge a compliment from him, if that's what he'd given me.

Dad stepped forward. "What do you want, Henry?"

"Someone in the county stealing calves again?" Mom
said.

"Maybe you heard the Wells girl was killed this morning," Moody said. "Murder. Robbery."

"We heard," Dad said.

"She had a party Saturday afternoon. Checking out all
the kids that were there. Takes lots of time." Moody turned
to me again, and the sun glinted off the cop's silver badge.
"Need you to answer some questions, Billy."

Dad said, "Billy's got nothing to do with robbery and
murder."

"Lord no," Mom said. "Not Billy."

"Just routine," Moody said. "Got to check everyone
out. You at the party, Billy?"

I nodded.

"How well did you know Lisa Wells?"

A sinking feeling in my stomach told me I'd never
be able to hide my sleeping with Lisa last night. Or all

the other times, either. Still, I had to try. I wasn't going to blurt out that kind of information without a struggle. Maybe I'd get lucky.

"We were friends," I said.

That wasn't a lie.

Mom piped in. "Would you like to come in for a cup of coffee? No use standing here in the drive."

Dad shot her a look. "The sheriff probably doesn't have time."

"I'll take a cup," Moody said.

"I'll make some," Mom said. "Got homemade pecan rolls, too. How about the other officers?"

They were leaning against their cruiser now, arms crossed. "No thanks, ma'am," they said. One was huge, nearly 250 pounds, I guessed. The other was tall and skinny.

"They can wait outside," Moody said.

"You're all welcome," Mom said, then hurried toward the house.

Moody said, "How good of friends, Billy?"

Good enough to sleep with whenever I wanted to for six weeks.

"We talked," I said.

I felt the cop's sharp eyes trying to dig inside my head. I looked away.

Moody said, "Lisa knew whoever robbed the place and killed her. No forced entry. No locks, doors, or windows broken. No smashed gun cases. Their doors were wide open, guns gone. No signs of a struggle. It was almost as if whoever done this had a key to the place. Or easy access."

Rodney Wells!

"Maybe the girl let him in," Dad said.

"Could be." Moody hooked his thumbs in his belt. "Billy, you shot trap at the party yesterday?"

I nodded.

"Folks I talked to already said you done good. Dr. Wells said you used a .20 gauge Browning Citori, over and under. Expensive gun. You broke twenty-five of twenty-five clay birds. Won seventy-five dollars on a bet. Did you like the gun?"

"Wait a minute!" Dad said.

Moody pursed his lips. "That gun your boy was using, Will, is one of them five guns stolen."

I stared at Moody. "I didn't steal any guns!"

Moody held up his hands. "Hold on a minute, Billy. I didn't say you did. Lots of confusing details in this case. I've got to consider all possibilities."

"Henry," Dad said, "I resent your coming on my place asking my son questions like that. He has nothing to do with this. He hardly knew the girl. Only went to school with her. Isn't that right, Billy?"

I swallowed again. I couldn't find any words that weren't a lie and that didn't sound incriminating.

"When did this robbery and murder happen?" Dad said.

"One AM this morning. That's when Dr. Wells heard

the shot. Whoever done it must've fled on foot. Dr. Wells didn't see a car drive away. The perpetrator must've parked along the road leading to the grounds."

Dad smiled, satisfied. "That ends this discussion. Billy was home sleeping. I can vouch for that."

I flinched. Looked at the ground. Said nothing.

"Coffee's ready," Mom called from the side door of the house.

I felt as if I'd tumbled into a bin of shelled corn, was sinking, and would soon suffocate.

———————————

Inside the house, Moody, Dad, and I sat at the kitchen table. Mom poured coffee for Moody, then Dad, its aroma filling the room. Finished with the coffee, she poured a glass of milk for me.

The other two cops remained outside.

Nobody was talking right now, and I was thankful for the silence.

Moody reached for a pecan roll, broke it in two, picked up a knife, and smeared butter on both halves.

"Thank you, Eileen," he said, his dark eyes admiring Mom again in her light blue Sunday-morning church dress.

If asked, I'd say she was the prettiest farm wife and mom in the county.

"Still a bachelor, I am," Moody said. "All I get is store-bought rolls."

The way Moody looked at Mom and the way Mom, Dad, and Moody used first names made me wonder if they knew each other from a long time ago. They all looked the same age, Mom a little younger.

I nibbled at a roll, took a deep swallow of cold milk, and studied Moody over the rim of the glass. With his dark eyes and eyebrows, chiseled features and mustache, he made me feel nervous and trapped.

I had one chance in a million to fight my way out of this.

"Have you talked to Rodney Wells?" I said. "Lisa's stepbrother."

"Funny about him," Moody said. "He seems to have disappeared."

"He must have a key to the house," I said. "Maybe keys to the gun cases. Lisa said he's always stealing things from her. He drinks and gambles. He needs the money. He's the guy I won seventy-five dollars from, shooting."

Moody nodded. "We'll find him."

"I'll bet he killed Lisa," I said. "She caught him stealing the guns. It all makes sense. That's got to be the way it happened."

Mom said, "Where'd you get that kind of money to bet, Billy?" She set the coffeepot back on the stove.

"I didn't have it," I said. "Didn't need it, anyway—I won."

"Did you collect?" Moody said.

"Uh-uh. After I finished shooting, I couldn't find Rodney. I'm sure he's your murderer."

Moody said, "Talked to Eric Benson this morning just before I came out to your place. Lisa's boyfriend. You know him?"

I shrugged. "A little."

"Says during the party he saw you in the house alone near the rec room, where the guns are."

"I was looking for a restroom—"

The instant I said that I bit my lip. I realized I might have made a major mistake.

"Dr. Wells provided Port-O-Potties outside," Moody said. "His and hers." Moody leveled his eyes on me. "Eric says you had more than a friendly interest in Lisa."

"Henry," Dad said, "what's the point of all these questions? Billy was home. Sleeping."

"Don't get excited, Will. Just trying to get the truth from Billy here, but he's not cooperating. Are you, Billy?"

Mom shot a questioning look at the cop. "Are you trying to accuse Billy of something, Henry?" She pulled out a chair and sat at the table.

"Might be."

Dad said, "Billy, have you lied to this man about anything?"

"Billy doesn't lie," Mom said. "I know that for a fact."

I felt sweat under my arms. I knew my face was ablaze— I heard my blood pounding in my ears.

Dad said, "Billy, tell Sheriff Moody whatever he wants to know so he can leave promptly."

Moody stared at me. "Let's start with the first question again, Billy. How well did you know Lisa Wells?"

My knees began shaking under the kitchen table. My folks would never trust me again. Never believe in me again.

"Answer him," Dad said.

"We were good friends."

"How good?" Moody asked.

My throat suddenly felt rusty. I coughed to clear it. "Very good."

Moody nodded. "According to Dr. Wells, last night about ten-twenty the newly installed motion lights on the underside of the deck round the second floor of his house went on. He thought an intruder set them off. Lisa told him she looked out the window of her bedroom when they came on and saw a couple of deer. You know what I think, Billy?"

Another swallow. Painful. I couldn't answer. My voice was hiding.

"I think an intruder set them lights off, Billy. Lisa Wells let that intruder into her bedroom and entertained him. Preliminary indications are she had sex with some-one before she was killed. The medical examiner will be able to tell us more. I think her and the intruder jumped into bed—"

"It was me," I said softly, wringing my hands. "I was there with Lisa."

Mom and Dad gasped and stared at me with disbelieving eyes.

"You?" Dad said.

"We made love," I said.

Mom's face turned red, then ashen, all the blood drained. I'd never seen her like that.

Dad stood, smacking his fist on the table, making the coffee cups jump. "I can't believe it! You were in this house, sleeping!"

Smiling, Moody leaned his chair back, balancing it on its two rear legs. "Figured it was you, Billy. We played the recording from Lisa Wells's answering machine. On it a voice says, 'It's me, Billy. I'll be there tonight.' Wasn't nobody else at the party named Billy." Moody hooked his thumbs in his belt again. "You were the last person to see her alive."

I gulped.

I felt like I was standing in the loft in the barn. Moody had slipped a noose around my neck and had thrown the loose end up over the rafters. He was getting ready to give me a big push. Hang me for a robbery and murder I didn't commit.

Twelve

Dad stood by the refrigerator, silent and stony, staring at me.

I glanced at him and tried to make my face say *I'm not guilty, I'm not guilty.* But his look cut so deep my chin dropped to my chest.

Fighting tears, Mom kept saying, "My Lord, Billy. What have you been doing? My Lord, Billy…"

"This can't be true," Dad said.

Moody eased the front legs of his chair down. He sipped his coffee, set the cup carefully on the saucer, and leaned across the table, closer to me.

I smelled the coffee on the cop's breath.

"You ready to tell me the truth, Billy?"

"I didn't kill her. I didn't steal the guns."

"No one said you did, Billy. Just tell me the truth. How and why did you end up last night in Lisa Wells's bed? Tell me everything. From the beginning."

I felt Mom's and Dad's eyes welded to me.

I told them and Moody about my getting to know Lisa when she started leaving notes in my locker. The first time we were alone I met her at Hollyhocks Park in Eldridge after school, and she invited me over Saturday night. I didn't know her dad was gone for the weekend. We made love. I admitted that for later meetings with Lisa I sneaked out of the house at night, canoed across the lake, and crept into her bedroom. We carried on like that for about six weeks, her dad sleeping in his bedroom below us.

I told them about last night. A little bit.

"How many other times?" Moody asked me.

"What difference does it make?"

"How many?"

"A few."

"The truth," Moody said. "The truth, Billy, is always better than a lie."

I chewed the side of my bottom lip. "Sixteen."

Mom gasped. Dad grunted.

Moody grinned. Nodded thoughtfully. "She was probably tired of you, you two fought—"

"She wasn't tired of me."

I finally glanced up to find Mom and Dad still staring at me. Their eyes looked huge and glassy. I wanted to disappear through the floor. They now knew I was not the person they thought me to be: chaste and honest.

"Let me get this straight," Moody said. "This beautiful, talented rich girl wanted you in the first place because…?"

"I don't know for sure. I think she thought I was…different from her other friends."

Moody pursed his lips. "I see…and yesterday at the party, after you hadn't been with her for a couple of weeks, she begged you to…visit her?"

"Something like that."

"She asked you to come see her because—help me here, Billy. What's the right word?"

"I don't know what you're trying to say."

"Because she was horny? Is that your story, Billy?"

I glared at the cop. "You don't know how her father manipulated her life—how she's wanted to get away from him. How lonely she was. How she wanted to be free. I went there last night to convince her that now that she was eighteen she could move out on her own."

"Not to have sex with her, though," Moody said. "That was an accident."

My face was a barn on fire.

Mom reached across the table and held my hand, tears on her cheeks. "Billy, Billy, Billy…what were you thinking? What have you done?"

Dad remained standing by the fridge, his burly arms crossed over his chest, his expression grim.

"I didn't raise him," Dad said, "to be sneaking out at night, carrying on, but he's my boy. If he says he didn't kill that girl and steal them guns, he didn't."

Moody let out a low breath. "Got a search warrant, Will. Had to get the judge out of bed early this morning. Hope you don't mind if my men look around a bit."

"Might as well. Nothing to hide here."

"I didn't steal anything," I said.

"I'll have them poke around outside first," Moody said. "Lots of places to hide guns on a farm. Barns, corn-cribs, haylofts. All kinds of places."

Taking a final bite of roll and the last sip of coffee, Moody shoved his chair back and rose from the table. "Be right back." He went to the door and stepped outside.

His face livid, Dad turned on me. "Are you telling me, behind our back, practically every night, you've been sneak-ing out of this house, to sleep with that girl?"

"Not every night."

"One night is too damn many!" he thundered.

"Will! Please…"

He said, "What kind of son does something like that? Can't you see the trouble you've gotten yourself into?"

"I didn't kill her. I didn't steal those guns."

Mom said, "Can't you see how wrong it is, what you've been doing, Billy?"

"Why?" Dad said. "I want to know *why?*"

Moody stepped into the kitchen, the screen door banging behind him. "My men are looking around." He handed Dad an envelope. "Search warrant in there," he said, "if you care to look at it." He touched his moustache. "Lisa was shot with a small-caliber handgun. You got handguns around the house, Will?"

"I have one." Dad tossed the envelope on the cupboard.

"I use it for target practice," I said. "A twenty-two pistol. That's all we've got."

"Mind if I have a look at it?"

"It's in my room," I said. "In the basement."

"Lead the way."

The steps to the basement were off the kitchen. I snapped on a light. Closing the door, Moody followed me down the stairs.

"Nice and private down here," he said. "Made it easy to sneak out at nighttime, didn't it?"

He was right about that, but I kept my mouth shut.

I opened the door to my room and flipped a switch, the room flooding with light from the ceiling. I watched Moody's eyes land instantly on the gun rack on the wall that cradled four shiny weapons: three shotguns and one high-powered rifle with a scope, all with trigger locks.

"Those are mine," I said. "I have a sales receipt for each one."

"Don't get excited, boy."

Moody's head moved slowly as his eyes took in the rest

of the room: the unmade double bed; cluttered dresser, a mirror above it; littered desk with a computer and printer on it; stereo and speakers; beige walls with posters of deer, pheasants, and quail; four fishing pools in the corner; jeans, socks, and sneakers strewn across the floor.

"Cozy," Moody said. "Your folks ever tell you that me, your mom, and your dad all went to high school together?"

"No. Why would they tell me that? Why would I care?" I pointed. "The twenty-two is in the closet. Over there."

"Get it for me." Then, "We were like best friends, your mom, dad, and me."

I ignored that. I couldn't figure out why he wanted me to know about their friendship.

I opened the door to a closet full of clothes hanging up and assorted sneakers and boots on the floor. On the top shelf, amid boxes of shotgun shells, old fishing reels, a bunch of battered board games, I pulled down a small black-leather case, almost the shape of a triangle.

"Here," I said.

"You sure that's the only handgun around here?"

I nodded.

Moody unzipped the case, checked to make sure the gun wasn't loaded, noted the trigger lock, then smelled the muzzle. "It's been fired recently."

"I target shoot a lot."

"Mind if I look around some more?"

"Go ahead."

"Got a ladder?" Moody flicked his head toward the

ceiling. "Removable ceiling tile. Nice place to hide guns, up in them rafters."

I stomped out of the room and dragged a stepladder out from under the basement steps. I could hear Mom and Dad talking upstairs, but with the stairway door closed I couldn't make out what they were saying. No doubt Dad was cussing me out, Mom telling him to keep his voice down.

The wooden six-foot ladder was dusty and musty-smelling. A black spider slithered down one side. I couldn't remember the last time the ladder had been used.

When I brought the ladder in, Moody was poking in the corners of the closet. "See you got a bow and arrows back there," Moody said. "You like weapons, don't you, boy?"

"You're wasting your time. You should be tracking down Rodney Wells."

Moody turned from the closet and smiled. "We'll find him."

Taking his flashlight from his belt, the cop got down on his hands and knees and searched under the bed, sweeping the light back and forth. He stood up and sighed. He poked his hands under the mattress on my bed. He searched from the head of the bed to the foot and all the way across. His hands came out with nothing. Not even a *Playboy*.

"Satisfied?" I said.

I heard the outside door open. Then the stairway door

opened. I stepped out of the bedroom, wondering if I was going to have to deal with two more cops trashing my private place.

A shaft of light spilled down the stairs from the open door at the top.

"Henry, you down there?" one of the cops shouted.

Moody huffed to the bedroom doorway. "What?"

"C'mon up here. We found something."

Moody brushed the dust from the ladder off his hands. "Found what?" he said, heading up the steps.

"A gun in the kid's pickup," the cop said. "A twenty-five-caliber Colt automatic. Fancy little thing."

In the cool morning sunshine, we all stood outside forming a circle next to my truck: three cops, Mom, Dad, and me. Still chained to his doghouse, Mallard barked at us.

Dad's lips had set themselves in a thin line. The cops looked smug and triumphant. Mom was pale as death, and I was numb, unable to believe my ears or eyes.

"Found it under the driver's seat," the thin cop said. The gun lay in its opened black-leather case. Moody held the case flat in the palm of his hand. "May be a collector's gun," he said. "Pretty pearl handle."

"Somebody...somebody put the gun there," I stammered. "I didn't."

Moody said, "Where'd you hide the other guns, Billy?"

"Why would I put that gun under the seat in my truck," I said, "and hide the others? Why not hide it, too?"

"Because it's such a pretty little thing," Moody said, "and you like guns and you target shoot. You were probably going shooting today." He jerked his head toward the other two cops. "Check out the house. The boy's got a bedroom in the basement. Check out the rafters above the ceiling tile. Copy down the serial numbers from them guns on the wall."

The cops nodded and turned toward the house, Mallard barking at them.

Dad said, "Only rifles and shotguns reported missing is what you told us. Are you saying the pistol belongs to this Dr. Wells? That it's the one used to kill his girl?"

"Don't know," Moody said. "But I'll have it checked out in no time."

"Somebody planted that gun," I said. "I didn't steal it or any other gun."

"We'll lift prints from it," Moody said. "Then we'll take yours, see if we get a match."

Dad glared at Moody. "Twenty years, you've finally found a way to get even, haven't you, Henry?"

"Has nothing to do with me and you, Will. This boy of yours is a murder and robbery suspect."

"He's innocent," Mom said.

"Hope you got money laid back," Moody said. "No mortgages on this farm. Billy's going to need a fancy lawyer."

"You swore you'd get even," Dad said.

Moody's cheek twitched. "Some things can't be forgotten, Will. Or forgiven."

"I didn't kill her," I said. "I didn't steal any guns."

"Henry, can't you see he's telling the truth?" Mom said.

"Like he came right out and told the truth about sleeping with the girl?" Moody said.

"He's my boy"—Dad's fists clenched—"and I'm standing by him." A fierce look buckled Dad's face, and his lips curled.

Moody's left hand touched the mace canister on his belt. "Don't make no mistakes, Will. Your boy's made enough already."

Sucking in a breath, Dad took a step toward Moody, but I stepped in front of Dad, held my ground, and Mom grabbed his arm.

"Will!" she said. "Don't!"

"Get off my place!" Dad shouted at Moody.

"Got a search warrant, Will. Remember? Soon's my men are finished, I'll be leaving."

At that moment the huge cop came out of the house, shaking his head. "Nothing."

The thin one followed, shrugging.

Moody looked disappointed but said, "Well, we got quite a bit, anyway. Two hand guns, one of which may be the murder weapon. Admission from Billy here he slept with the girl before she died."

"Doesn't mean I killed her," I said.

Moody nodded. "I'll tell you right now, Will, it'll go easier on your boy if he tells me where them other guns are."

"I don't know," I said. "Someone else put that pistol in my truck. Why would I be stupid enough to steal it and leave it under the seat?"

"You've done some other stupid things," Moody said.

"You heard him," Dad said to Moody. "He doesn't know. Now get off my place and don't come back."

Moody stroked his mustache. "Oh, I'll be back, Will. Kids keep killing kids all over the country—I'll have no more of it in my county, though. I'll be back, I'll be back to take this boy with me in cuffs. Get him a lawyer."

Thirteen

"Why?" Dad said. "*Why?*"

Mom said, "How *could* you, Billy?"

Their looks alternated between exasperation and anguish.

I shook my head, my face feeling crimson again.

I'd gone to my room to change out of my Sunday clothes. Mom and Dad had changed, too. I was the last one to return to the kitchen.

Mom was mixing flour in a bowl with eggs, milk, and water. Pork sausages sizzled in an iron skillet on the stove.

Dad sat at the table, drinking coffee, the Sunday morning paper spread open in front of him on the table. He was reading in the sports pages about Lisa's attending SCU to play volleyball. He hardly ever read sports.

Waffles and sausage are what my folks and I have every Sunday morning for breakfast after church. Mom and Dad's daily, monthly, and yearly routines sometimes seemed carved in stone.

I hoped I'd grow up to be a little more free-spirited.

I wasn't hungry this morning. I didn't know if I'd ever be hungry again. No part of me believed this was happening.

I was ashamed that I'd deceived Mom and Dad, and I was terrified because I knew Moody would try his hardest to convict me of robbery and murder. He wouldn't want to lose his reputation for being a tough sheriff who jumped on teen violence immediately. Besides, I think he hated my dad. No, I *knew* he hated my dad. What was that all about?

"I'm sorry," I said. "I never meant for any of this to happen."

"Sit down," Dad said. He seemed a bit calmer. "I want you to tell me again exactly what's been going on. And why."

I pulled out a chair and sat, elbows on the table. "You heard me tell Moody. I'd been seeing Lisa at night."

"Sneaking out of the house?"

"Yes."

"My Lord," Mom said, and poured several ladles full of batter onto the automatic waffle iron, lowering the lid. "Didn't you realize that was wrong? Didn't you realize how dangerous that could be? If her father had caught you, what would he have done?"

Dad said, "Why, Billy?"

That was the hard one. I rubbed the back of my neck. "Because…she liked me. I mean, I'm a farm kid—"

"What's wrong with that?" Mom said.

"But she liked me. The university president's daughter, she liked me. She snubbed her other friends because she was looking for someone different."

"And you had sex with her?" Dad said. "Every time?"

"Yes." Hardly a whisper.

"Your being farm-raised," Mom said, "nothing wrong with that." She rolled the sausages over in the skillet and they sizzled louder. "You should be proud."

"Mom, I am, but to think that the university president's daughter hit on me—it was so amazing. So unexpected."

Dad cleared his throat. "You're telling me the gospel truth? You did not steal those guns? Or kill that girl?" Dad's head waggled. "Sweet Jesus! I never dreamed I'd be asking my son questions like this."

"I had nothing to do with any of it, Dad."

"How'd that gun find its way into your truck?" Mom said.

"The person," I said, "who killed Lisa probably put it there, someone who knows about Lisa and me and thinks I'd be an easy person to frame."

Dad nodded.

"First waffle will be ready soon," Mom said, and I

smelled its sweet aroma as she opened the griddle, but my appetite still didn't kick in.

"Who thinks you'd be easy to frame?" Dad said.

"Rodney Wells." I explained about Lisa's stepbrother, his gambling and drinking problem, his stealing from the family. "Or maybe Moody himself," I said, suddenly wondering if an accusation like that wasn't too far off.

Dad looked surprised.

Mom said, "Him?"

"He knows about Lisa and me," I said. "He could've taken that gun from Dr. Wells's house. Planted it. He doesn't like me, and he doesn't like Dad. That's not hard to tell." I looked at Dad. "I heard you tell Moody he'd finally found a chance to get even. What's that all about?"

Mom and Dad flicked each other a glance. But neither said a word.

I broke the silence with, "He said all you guys went to high school together." I halted, waiting.

"He told you that?" Dad said

Mom took a breath. "When did he say that?"

"When we were in the basement, and he was searching my room."

Dad laced his fingers. "What else did he say?"

"Just that you guys were in high school together. All of you were best friends."

Opening the griddle, Mom speared the steaming waffle with a fork and set it on a plate in front of Dad, her hand trembling. "Forgot butter and syrup."

"What happened?" I said.

"It was a long time ago." Mom reached for syrup in the cupboard. "No one talks about it anymore, but if you want to know—"

Dad's head eased up. "Enough," he said quietly, and Mom clammed up as she set the syrup on the table.

I blew out a long breath.

Dealing with Moody, being accused of murder and robbery, making a confession about Lisa and me, witnessing my folks' sudden secretiveness—I couldn't handle any of it any longer.

My eyes turned watery, and suddenly Mom's and Dad's faces blurred. I rose shakily, my chair legs scraping across the kitchen floor. Rather than eating, I felt like throwing up.

Mom said, "Sit down, Billy. Here's butter."

"I'm not hungry," I said.

"Stay right here and eat!" Dad said.

"Not this morning." I wobbled across the kitchen and out of the house, slamming the door closed behind me.

Fourteen

Teeth clenched, I crunched the gas pedal to the floor. The pickup's tires ripped into the gravel road in front of the house, spitting rocks, and created the inevitable cloud of dust.

I didn't know where I was going, what I was going to do.

I'd unchained Mallard. He sat next to me in the front seat, panting, tongue hanging out of his mouth.

I was guilty of deceiving my parents and Windy and having sex with a beautiful girl. But not robbery. Not murder.

As the pickup hurdled down the gravel road, its wheels bucked over potholes, and I gripped the steering wheel harder to keep the vehicle from catapulting into a ditch.

I glanced at the speedometer. *Seventy-five.* My stomach tightened. *Eighty.*

The gravel dust whipped in through the pickup's rolled-down windows and swirled inside the vehicle, hitting me in the face. My eyes felt gritty and suddenly turned watery. I squinted. The curve ahead was a blur.

A voice in the back of my head screamed: "*Slow down! This is stupid! You'll kill yourself!*"

I held my breath and slammed down on the brakes. The tires locked, chewed gravel, and the pickup skidded. I felt Mallard fly across the seat, crash off the passenger's door, then slam off me. As the pickup spun, I whipped the wheel around. Suddenly the vehicle lurched to a halt, pointed in the direction I'd just come from. Home.

I pulled in a sharp breath, inhaling dust, coughing.

Mallard licked my ear.

I scratched his nose. "Sorry, pal. Didn't mean to throw you around like that."

I closed my eyes, gripped the wheel at the top, and lowered my head, resting it on the back of my hands.

There's got to be an answer. And I've got to find it. Quick. Before I'm hauled off to jail. I won't even have a chance to graduate.

Mallard whined and licked my ear once more.

———————

Windy was finishing washing the family minivan. The vehicle was parked under a maple tree in the front yard of her house. It was nearly noon, the sun nailed almost straight overhead in a clear sky. At the sight of Windy and water, Mallard started barking.

I opened the passenger's door and said, "Go!"

Mallard bounded onto the lawn, and Windy blasted him with a full spray from the hose. He romped back and forth in twenty-yard sweeps. Windy aimed the spray so it hit him in the head and the shoulders.

After she'd doused Mallard, she turned the hose off, set it down, and strolled around to my side of the pickup. She was barefoot. Mallard halted and shook himself off.

"Afraid to get out?" she said.

"No."

"If you sent Mallard to get back in my good graces, it won't work."

The white T-shirt she wore tucked into cutoff jeans was wet in front and clung to her breasts.

"I need your help," I said.

"Cops come by?"

My fingers flexed on the steering wheel. "Want to drive out to the quarry and fish a bit?"

Windy looked in the bed of the pickup. "No poles."

"I was in a hurry when I left."

"What did the cops say?"

"Get two poles and your tackle box."

"Wrong time of day to go fishing."

"You want to know what the cops said?"

"Wait till I rinse the car off."

The Dewey Portland Cement Company abandoned the Atalissa limestone quarry over fifty years ago. As big as a city block, in a hollow surrounded by tall trees, the quarry is said to be seventy-five, maybe one hundred feet deep. When Windy and I arrived, its blue-green water sparkled in the afternoon sunshine, smelling clean and fresh.

There's a shallow side to the quarry with a rocky shore and a lot of scruffy weeds growing. You can walk up the water's edge and see a million tiny bluegills darting around. The other side of the quarry is a limestone wall maybe thirty feet high with tall trees growing at the top. You can follow a path around the quarry, reach the limestone wall, and jump or dive into the water.

If you're brave enough.

Windy and I'd been diving here since I was fourteen. A year younger than me, she was thirteen when she made her first dive. I have to admit she did it before I did. Gathering the courage to follow her took me a week. I must admit, also, the first time I sailed off the ledge, I didn't dive like Windy had—I jumped.

Last summer when we'd come to spend a sun-baked afternoon diving and swimming, a strange thing happened between Windy and me. On our last dive of the afternoon,

I went first and then swam across the quarry to the shallow side, Windy following me.

On shore, I turned and looked for her. I didn't see her for a second, and my heart got all panicky. Then she surfaced. I yelled, "What's wrong?"

"Nothing," she called back, and started swimming toward me.

By the time she reached shore, I could tell what was wrong, all right. I didn't know what to do—I didn't dare laugh. Stifling a smirk, I held a hand out to help her step across the rocky bottom but kept my mouth shut. Just held my breath and felt my heart beat faster, my face getting hot.

"Lost my top," Windy said matter-of-factly, then smiled. The sun glinted off her wet, black hair. "Mom said it was too small." She clutched the skimpy, yellow, wadded-up top in her right fist. "Had to swim around and find it."

"Nice tits," I blurted, the words startling me. I gulped. I'd never said anything like that to a girl before.

Windy tilted her head, and glanced at me from the corner of her eyes. "Think so?"

"Yeah."

"Never thought you'd notice."

She drew in a breath. Her brown eyes locked with mine a moment. In my brain, I caught a flash of—what? Desire? Lust? *Oh, wow!* Was I seeing the same emotions reflected back from her eyes?

I gulped again.

The moment was like none other we'd ever shared.

Suddenly Windy dashed over to her towel and clothes lying on a big rock and flung herself into a super-long white T-shirt that fell all the way to her bottom, covering it. Almost.

The sight of her topless, her acting so cool—I mean, she could've crossed her arms—all of it, like, weirded me out and gave me a feeling for her I'd never felt before, a pull toward her that I could barely resist.

As we picked up our towels, picnic basket, and empty pop cans, I made myself stop looking at her—barelegged and braless under her T-shirt.

We hardly spoke on the way home. Had something happened between us? What?

I thought of the Garden of Eden story. Adam and Eve. But Windy and I hadn't seen a snake nor eaten an apple.

I dwelled on the incident that night in bed for a long while. In my mind, I could still see her topless, nipples pumped. Incredible. But this wasn't right. Windy was a buddy. You snapped a buddy on the butt in a locker room with a towel and laughed. You didn't suddenly lust for your buddy on a summer afternoon and long to drag her into the tall grass.

We never mentioned the incident. No need to. I figured out after awhile that Windy had walked out of the water bare-topped on an impulse. She was like that. No need for me to ask, "What was that all about?" or for her to get all embarrassed trying to explain, maybe even apologize.

So I brushed the incident aside, but maybe it had meant more to us than I'd realized.

––––––––––

At the water's edge now, as Windy was tying a lure onto the end of her line, I gave the pole she'd loaned me a wrist-flick and lofted a green and yellow spinner bait thirty yards out into the water. It landed with a splash.

Windy was right. This wasn't the best time of day to fish, especially for bass, but I didn't care. This was a perfect way to calm down and to get my thoughts together.

On the way to the quarry, I'd told her about the cops' visit to my house and their finding a twenty-five-caliber automatic in my pickup under the seat. She listened silently.

Now she said, "Why would the cops think you killed Lisa? That doesn't make sense."

Mallard stood in the water up to his chest, lapping.

"They think because I shot so well with that Browning, I went back to steal the guns, and she caught me. I killed her." I reeled in my bait with a steady motion. "They think I hid the guns except for the pistol. I put it in the pickup because I was going to target shoot somewhere. But they don't even know if the pistol belongs to Dr. Wells or not."

"That's stupid," Windy said. "A little gun like that's no fun to target shoot with, anyway."

"Even if it belongs to Dr. Wells, they'll be disappointed when they don't find my fingerprints on it."

Pole in hand, Windy climbed up a limestone ledge six feet above the water and cast a black and gold spinner bait. "But because they found a pistol in your pickup—which anybody could've put there, which may or may not be connected with the murder—they're convinced you did it."

"There's something else," I said.

"What?"

I knew if I was going to earn Windy's confidence back, I couldn't lie to her ever again. Same with my parents.

I jerked back on my pole, thinking I'd felt a hit, but there was nothing on the line. I inhaled, exhaled.

"I slept with her last night."

Windy whirled around on the ledge to stare at me, her face crumbling. "You what?"

"Be careful. You're going to fall in."

"You slept with her!"

"Yes."

She wound up like a javelin thrower and hurled her pole at me, handle first. I ducked as the pole whizzed by my head, trailing line all the way from the ledge, across the ground, to where it landed in the dirt and grass.

"Are you crazy?" I said. "That's expensive gear you're throwing around."

Windy planted her feet apart on the limestone ledge, fists jammed into her waist. "Talk about crazy! You couldn't leave her alone, could you?"

"I'm sorry," I said.

"One smell of her at the party and you went crawling

back. I can*not* believe you! You are"—she shook her head in rage—"such a stupid—*dickhead!*"

My face turned hot.

Leaning my pole against a tree, I trotted over and picked up Windy's off the ground.

"I'm through with you." She stomped down from the ledge. "I don't care what happens to you. This time I'm totally through with you."

She brushed by me, angry tears in her eyes, and plunked down on the truck's open tailgate, arms crossed.

After seething for a moment, breathing hard, shaking her head, she said, "How did the cops figure out you slept with her?"

I shrugged. "I called her, left a message and my name on her answering machine. Said I'd be there."

"Jesus," Windy said in disbelief. "Was it worth it? That's all she ever wanted from you, you know. She used you! She made a fool of you!"

"I know."

"You let her! That's the worst part. That's what I can't stand. You let her!"

I climbed to the top of the ledge with Windy's pole and began reeling in her line. Mallard followed and peered over the ledge, his ears perked. He loved pouncing on a three-pound bass as well as a pheasant, duck, or quail. But there was nothing on the line this time.

I cast the bait out, reeled slowly, and glanced back at Windy. Arms still crossed, biting her bottom lip, she peered at the sky and trees. She was fighting her anger. I looked away.

I cast and reeled in again.

"It gets worse," I said.

"How could it?"

"My dad and Moody went to school together. For some reason, I think they hate each other. Moody'd like to nail my ass to the barn door to get back at Dad for something."

"You're in serious trouble, Billy."

"I know."

Windy stabbed at her tears with her fingers. "Who put that stupid gun in your pickup, that's what you've got to find out. Anybody who knows where you live could've done it."

"Moody or Rodney." I reeled in Windy's black and gold spinner bait, casting again. "Take your pick."

"Moody?"

"He could've," I said.

"Does Rodney know where you live?"

"I'm not sure."

"Eric knows."

"I hadn't thought of him."

"Did you watch him at the party yesterday?" Windy shook her head. "Of course not. You were too busy."

"What about him?"

"He was really bummed. He just stood around watching

everyone else having fun, talked to no one. Then sometimes he'd sneak off."

"When he got in my face, first thing at Lisa's party, I smelled booze on his breath."

"I'm not surprised."

"And when I was looking for Rodney, I found him in the house. I think maybe he was stealing booze from Dr. Wells."

"Our student body president is obviously not the perfect kid."

"But he's the guy Dr. Wells approves of. Unbelievable."

"You think he could've killed Lisa?" Windy said.

"Lisa and Eric went to a movie last night after the party. I'll bet they had a fight."

"Maybe because she invited you to the party. So after the movie, he took her home, went off, drank some more, then called her and staggered back to her house after you'd left. She let him in. He fought with her and killed her."

I nodded. "He'd seen me shoot and knew I liked that Browning. He stole the guns and hid the pistol under the seat in my pickup. A perfect way to get even with me for stealing Lisa."

"You need to talk to Eric Benson."

"The police already have."

"So what? They don't know half as much about Lisa and Eric as we do."

I reeled the spinner bait in, hooked it to an eye in the pole, then shuffled down from the ledge to my pickup.

Mallard barked, apparently unable to believe we were going to leave without a fish.

At the pickup I said, "I'm sorry I disappointed you. I know I'm an embarrassment to everyone."

"Embarrassment? What an understatement."

"I can't imagine what my folks must think of me. What you think."

"I already told you what I think. You're a *dickhead!*"

"Look," I said. "She dazzled me. I thought maybe she loved me. I was thrilled just to be in her life. I…I don't know…Have you ever felt like that about someone?"

Windy stiffened. She gave me a hard look through glassy eyes. "Once maybe," she said. "I hope the feeling goes away soon."

Guilt sliced me in two. "Windy—"

I carefully set the pole I was holding in the truck and reached for her hand, but she slapped mine away. "You're a *dickhead*, remember? And I'm still going to be pissed at you for the rest of your life."

"I'm sorry if I hurt you, I really am."

"Don't flatter yourself, Billy." Then, "Let's find out what Eric Benson knows."

Fifteen

"I'll tell Eric you're here," Mrs. Benson said.

"We'd appreciate that," Windy said.

"He's not been feeling well since...what happened."

I stood behind Windy on the screened-in front porch of Eric Benson's house and promised myself I wouldn't let Eric upset me. Shaded by maple trees, the porch was cool. I hoped I could stay that way.

Mallard sat patiently in the bed of my truck.

Eric lived in a wooded subdivision of State Center called Sherwood Forest, where the houses are sprawling, the watered green lawns neatly manicured. It's where many of the university professors live. Maples and oaks shade the houses, lawns, and sculptured shrubs. At least two shiny cars sat parked in each drive. An RV or a cruiser-type boat, sometimes both, lounged on a cement slab alongside nearly every house.

"Let me do the talking," Windy said, after Mrs. Benson left.

"Eric's not going to tell us anything."

"He might if you don't get him ticked off."

"'I killed Lisa'—is he going to say that?"

"Shhhh!" Windy hissed.

"If he says one thing about my staying on the farm—"

"Shut up, I hear someone!"

We waited a second.

Eric opened the screen door and pushed his glasses up his nose, covering puffy eyes. He looked beat. He stepped onto the screened-in porch and scowled. "Mom said two friends wanted to talk to me. She didn't mention you, Billy."

"Two of Lisa's friends."

Windy burned me with a look, then stepped in front of me, facing Eric, cutting me off from him.

"Look, Eric," she said, "let's try to be cool. We just want to talk."

"Nothing to talk about. Lisa's dead. Someone shot her."

I said, "Tell us what you know about it."

Windy elbowed me a good one in the ribs. "We're trying," she said calmly, "to figure out what really happened. We don't think the cops know."

"Someone shot her and stole her Dad's guns; that's what happened."

"But who shot her?" Windy said.

"You know anything," I said, "about a gun? A twenty-five-caliber automatic, pearl handle?"

"What are you guys?" Eric said. "Amateur detectives? The police have already been here."

"They search your house?" I said.

"Yeah. They searched it, looking for the guns. We don't have any guns in this house, and I have an alibi."

"What?" Windy said.

"Why tell you?"

"Something to hide?" I said.

Eric scowled at me. "If you want to know, I got home at ten-thirty. I fell asleep in the house on the floor, watching TV. My parents found me when they came home at 1:00 AM, got me up, and made me go to bed." Eric whipped off his glasses and rubbed his eyes. "What's your alibi, Billy? You like guns."

"So what?"

"You're a regular Billy the Kid with a gun. You could've killed Lisa and stolen those guns."

"But I didn't."

"He was home, too," Windy said.

Her quick lie of support surprised me. Pleased me.

Tears misted in Eric's eyes. He wiped them quickly away with the heel of his hand. "Why didn't you leave Lisa alone?" he said to me.

"She came after me, I didn't chase her."

"That's a lie!"

"It's true," Windy said.

"You ruined everything for us," Eric said.

"Ruined it for *you* maybe," Windy said.

I waved a hand. "What? What did I ruin?"

"We had our summer planned. Sort of our last fling. Then she'd go off to college wherever, and I'd end up at Michigan. Then you started sniffing around. And then she dumps me for six weeks or so…and then she takes me back…and then last night…"

"What?" Windy said. "What about last night?"

"I don't want to talk about it."

"What?" I said.

"She was always unpredictable," Eric said, "but after you wormed your way into her life, I could never figure her out."

"Why were you so bummed at the party yesterday?" Windy said. "I watched you a couple of times."

"You were full of booze, too," I said.

Eric rubbed his face with both hands. "The night before the party Lisa gave me an eight-by-ten graduation picture and signed it, 'Best friends forever…' I was more than her best friend—and she knew it. She hung her state championship medal around the picture by its ribbon and gave both of them to me."

Eric's thick glasses magnified the tears in his eyes. He looked away, and suddenly silence washed over all of us.

Taking off his glasses again, he said, "I told her last night I'd drop my plans to go to Michigan—I don't care what my parents said—so I could go to school here and be with her."

"You would've done that?" Windy said.

"She wouldn't even let me talk about it, and when I took her home she said she was giving me a final kiss goodbye."

I could only stand frozen to the spot, my heart barely beating.

"She said that?" I managed. "A kiss goodbye?"

"I don't know why I'm telling you guys this." Eric slammed his glasses back on his face. "Get the hell out of here. Leave me alone."

"All right," Windy said. "We'll go."

"Look, man," I said, and took an awkward step forward. "I know exactly how you feel. I'm bummed, too. Lisa was…special." I held out my hand. "Maybe we can't be friends, but we should stick together so this thing gets solved—that's more important. A truce? Shake?"

"Go feed the pigs."

Spinning on his heels, Eric headed into the house. I reached to grab him by the back of the neck, whirl him back around, and punch his face in, but Windy pushed me toward the porch door.

"No, Billy! You're not starting more trouble."

———————

"You believe Eric's alibi?" I said.

After leaving Eric's, we stopped at the Tastee-Freez, a roadside hamburger-and-malt stand on the blacktop just outside Parkview. Windy'd said she was hungry.

I thought I was too upset to eat—Eric's final remark hadn't helped—but when I jumped out of the truck, the breeze carried the smell of sizzling hamburgers and French fries and awakened my appetite.

"You believe Eric's alibi?" I asked again.

"His is as good as yours, and we both know how good yours is."

"Thanks."

I ordered burgers, fries, and shakes for Windy and me. We sat outside at a round white table in the shade of a fluttering yellow umbrella.

Mallard sat between us on the concrete patio, thumping his tail, begging with eager eyes for a snack.

"I don't like Eric much," I said, "but I don't think he did it. And I feel for him." I slipped Mallard a French fry slopped with catsup. "He seems really shook."

"He's smart. He could be faking it. Wait till he finds out you slept with her the night she was killed."

"You going to tell him?"

"No. But the cops might."

Mallard whined and Windy held out three French fries for him. He licked them out off her hand with a single swipe of his tongue.

Then Windy fired another question at me: "Were you in love with Lisa?"

The question jolted me a little. To avoid answering, I bit into my burger and chewed. Windy waited. Eventually I had to stop chewing and swallow.

Finally I said, "Yes…at least I thought so." I shrugged. "I don't know…can you be in love with a person who doesn't love you back?"

Windy shot me an odd look. "I'm not sure."

"Lisa wasn't in love with me, I don't think. At least, she never said it, and it doesn't seem to me real love can be one-sided. It's got to be a two-way deal. Fifty-fifty."

"I told you, she was using you."

Time for my question: "Were you in love with Roger?"

"Hell, no. But I thought I was, at first. Just like you thought you might be in love with Lisa."

"Why'd you hook up with him?"

"He was a senior, I was a stupid sophomore. I made a mistake once, but I didn't keep going back to him."

"I must be beyond stupid."

"That's true." Then Windy rattled her ice cubes around in the bottom of her drink. Sucked in a sip through her straw. "Lisa dumped you and she dumped Eric. I wonder what she was going to do next?"

"I don't know. I remember she said she wasn't going to please her Dad any longer."

"What did she mean by that?"

"I don't know that either. And she told me she wasn't going to hang with Eric all summer before he went off to Michigan."

"What was she going to do, suddenly become celibate?"

"Maybe."

Windy gave a snort. "Are you kidding? I doubt if she could go very long without some guy in her bed."

"She said Eric wasn't good for her."

"That's strange. I thought they were the perfect couple—two spoiled rich kids."

I wanted to defend Lisa, but instead I leaned back in my chair and kept my mouth shut.

Windy's lips curled around a French fry. "Remember yesterday I told you I was on the deck when I spotted you running out of the woods?"

"I remember."

"When Lisa came out of the woods and I saw she was headed for the deck, I waited for her at the bottom of the steps and told her to get out of your life, leave you alone."

"You told her that?"

"She told me not to worry. Soon I could have you all to myself—not that you're what I want."

I heaved out a sigh.

Windy said, "Why didn't she want you any longer?"

"She knew because of her dad's interference, a relationship between her and me would never work."

"Right. So she simply wanted you last night for another notch on her already carved-up bedpost. One last time."

I rolled my eyes at that, and we ate for a while in silence.

Windy wiped her mouth with a napkin. "Semester

evaluations next week. Tomorrow's Memorial Day, and I've got to study all day."

"Me, too—I won't be able to concentrate."

Windy scratched Mallard behind the ears and gave him three more French fries, one at a time.

"Want to know something else strange?" I said.

"What?"

"I saw Ms. Jameison after church this morning. She said Friday after school Lisa came to her house to talk and gave her the MVP trophy she'd won at state."

"Gave it to her?"

"Said she wanted Ms. Jameison to have it. Keep it."

"Like she gave her medal to Eric? And her picture?"

"That's right. You don't suppose…?"

"What?" Windy said.

I looked away. The thought that flashed through my brain gave me the shivers. "Never mind. It's a stupid idea."

"What? I hate it when people do that, start to say something and don't finish it."

I shook my head again, dismissing the half-formed notion. "I wish I knew where Rodney Wells is."

"What do you know about Rodney? Did Lisa ever talk about him?"

"Dr. Wells's first marriage was to a very rich widow with a little boy, Rodney. Lisa said his mom died in a boating accident…Dr. Wells had already adopted the kid."

"I'll bet he regretted that."

"No doubt."

"What about Lisa's mom? Where does she fit in?"

"Lisa would never talk about her mom. I got the feeling she's dead, but I'm not sure."

"We should find somebody who really knows Rodney Wells. Knows who his friends are. Where he hangs out. If Eric didn't kill Lisa, Rodney's the only other suspect."

"Except me," I said.

Sixteen

As Windy and I stood on Dr. Wells's front porch, ringing the chimes, my mouth turned dry.

"Suddenly I don't like this idea," I said, and took a calming breath. "Dr. Wells hates me."

"He's the only person we know who knows anything about Rodney."

I pushed the chime button again, turned, and looked down at the lake, sparkling in the afternoon sun. A breeze blew off the water, carrying a fresh-air scent. My eyes scanned the yard. The tent and tables were gone. The volleyball net and the horseshoe stakes were gone. The grass was almost trampled to dirt where kids had played games, celebrating Lisa's birthday.

Today everyone was mourning her death.

Was the killer mourning her death, too, realizing he'd done a terrible thing? Or was he celebrating, joyous because he was still unidentified?

Mallard watched us from the cab of my truck. I'd put him there because I was afraid that if a squirrel, rabbit, or some other varmint wandered out of the woods the dog would jump out of the truck bed and give chase. Or Lisa's cat, Muffin, might stroll by. Mallard hated cats.

"Someone's coming," Windy said.

My heart leapt into my throat.

Dr. Wells answered the door, a drained look in his eyes. I'd hoped a servant or a maid would answer and tell us Dr. Wells was not accepting visitors.

"What do you two want?" Dr. Wells said. His face was pale and slack, his voice flat.

"Could we talk for a minute?" Windy said.

Dr. Wells turned on me, and suddenly his weary eyes were hard, his face tense. "I can't believe you'd come back here."

"Dr. Wells," I said, "I didn't harm Lisa. I was here last night, I admit that, but—"

"You broke into my daughter's room. You violated her. You killed her. You stole—"

I cut him off. "I did *not* do any of those things, Dr.

Wells. Lisa invited me here. I left her alive. I didn't steal your guns."

Dr. Wells took a deep breath. "You have no idea how I worked and planned for her future." He glared at me. "I wanted her life to be limitless. You destroyed everything!"

"I didn't kill her!" I said, a wetness suddenly stinging my eyes. "I'm sorry for sneaking into your house, for sleeping with her. I know all that was wrong..." My voice faltered.

"You've got to help us find the real killer," Windy said.

Dr. Wells's eyes remained riveted on me. "The police called me this afternoon. They said they'd recovered a pistol of mine—found it under the front seat of your truck."

"It was your pistol?" I said.

"Yes, mine! Don't feign innocence." Dr. Wells's baritone voice was regaining its strength. "A twenty-five-caliber automatic with a pearl handle. I kept it in my desk drawer. I didn't realize it was stolen, too."

Windy said, "Someone put that gun in Billy's truck."

"If I stole it," I said, "I wouldn't be dumb enough to leave it in my tuck. Someone's trying to frame me."

"If I had done what you've done," Dr. Wells said, "I'd be saying the same thing."

"Who are Rodney's friends?" Windy said.

Dr. Wells swung his gaze toward her and then jerked his chin at me. "Why are you associating with him? You're a decent young girl. I've seen you play ball. You have potential, too."

"He's…my friend." Windy swallowed, as if the words had left a bitter taste in her mouth.

"He's dangerous," Dr. Wells said. "Your life is at risk. He cannot deny what he did to Lisa."

"I deny everything except caring for her," I said.

I felt a cool breeze blowing in from off the lake and hitting me on the back. But the breeze wasn't enough to stop sweat from beading on my upper lip.

"Look," Windy said to Dr. Wells, "maybe we can find out the truth if you can tell us who Rodney's friends are. We think maybe he's involved."

"The police have already talked to me about Rodney."

I swiped a fingertip across my upper lip. I tried to breathe evenly. "He could've come back here last night to steal the guns—he needed money. Lisa told me he'd stolen things from her and from the house. He probably knew where the pistol was. Lisa caught him in the middle of the robbery."

"He hasn't been here since yesterday."

"He killed her. He didn't like me and thought leaving the pistol under the seat in my truck would be a sure way to throw the police off."

Windy nodded. "Where does he hang out when he's home from college?"

I watched Dr. Wells's hand sneak around to grip the doorknob on the inside of the door, I think. Like he was getting ready to slam the door on Windy and me. Slam it right in our faces.

He said, "You have no authority to question me."

"Give us one name," Windy said. "A person. A place. It might lead to other names and eventually we might find Rodney."

"Lisa's killer is standing right in front of me." Dr. Wells pointed a trembling finger at me. "And I'll see to it you hang for Lisa's death."

"Something strange was going on in her life," Windy said.

"Want to hear something really strange?" I said. "She was giving away medals and awards she'd won for playing volleyball."

"Leave the premises. Now!"

"How many medals, plaques, and trophies did she give away?" I said.

"I'll call the police if you don't leave immediately!"

"Lisa has a trophy case in the living room," I said, "filled with volleyball awards she's won since sixth grade." I took a step toward the door. "I'd like to see what's missing."

Dr. Wells let go of the doorknob. He stepped in front of me and grabbed my shoulders. A powerful man with plenty of upper body strength, he thrust me back. "Get out of here! I'll have you arrested for trespassing—I don't know why you aren't in jail now." His face was red with rage. He stood poised in front of the door, his fists clenched.

Windy practically jumped on my back and wrapped her arms around me, probably thinking I might charge him. "Don't, Billy!"

I shrugged her off and stepped back from Dr. Wells. "It's all right," I said. "It's all right—I think I know what's happening here."

Windy and I sat at the kitchen table at her house. She was talking on the phone.

I poured Coke from a plastic liter bottle over two glasses full of ice. Her parents had gone to the annual Memorial Day Firemen's Picnic.

Mallard was tied outside with a rope to the apple tree in the backyard. He was barking at Calico, Windy's cat, which sat on the bottom step of the back porch, four feet outside the dog's reach, tail swishing, teasing him.

Windy stabbed the OFF button on the cordless phone.

"That's it," she said, and set the phone on the table. "I talked to six girls on the volleyball team. The others weren't home. Five of six I talked to said Lisa hadn't given them a gift. They thought I was weird for asking. Lindsay Wilson said that Friday Lisa gave her a trophy she had won for being the league's most valuable player when they played together on a seventh grade team and won the city championship."

"Were Lindsay and Lisa good friends?"

"The best. They'd played every game together since junior high."

"Lisa gave gifts to people she liked or felt she owed."

"We all know what she gave you."

I ignored that and said, "Did you see how alarmed Dr.

Wells got when I mentioned Lisa's giving things away? He knew I was beginning to suspect"—I hated to say it— "suicide."

"I never thought of suicide," Windy said. "But it does make sense."

"I thought about it for half a second when we were eating lunch, but the idea didn't make real sense until we started talking to Dr. Wells."

"The more I think about it...the more reasonable it sounds."

"I wrote a term paper last semester for psych class about suicide. People often give things away. Lisa gave Ms. Jameison a trophy. Eric, a picture and medal. Lindsay, a trophy."

"She sort of gave you away to me. Like a trophy."

I shook my head and wondered if Windy would ever let up. Probably not. Whatever she threw at me I deserved.

"Did she ever give a hint?" Windy said. "You know, like, 'I hate my life, I'm tired of living.'"

"Remember, she told me she was tired of pleasing her dad—she wasn't going to please him anymore."

"That could've been a hint."

A shiver rippled through me. "Wait! I remember her saying she'd rather die than go to college here."

Windy nodded slowly. "She probably meant it."

"I should've been listening to her every word. Figuring things out."

I closed my eyes a moment and pictured Lisa and me

together in her bedroom last night. I heard her voice. Felt her touch. Smelled her scent. *You should've been there for her, Billy.*

"This wasn't your fault," Windy said. "Don't start feeling guilty."

"I can't help it."

"Relax. Concentrate on what we're trying to figure out here."

"All right."

"If what we're thinking is true, it means our suspicions about Rodney are pointless. Instead of looking for a killer, we should be looking for—what?"

I rubbed my forehead. "Maybe a suicide note. A note to prove there was no murder."

"Suicides don't always leave notes, do they?"

"Not always. Lisa wrote a lot, though. She filled the school magazine with her poems and stories. Her art work, too."

"Then who's framing you?" Windy flopped back in her chair. "And what's the point in framing you? In the movies they always make a murder look like a suicide. Who'd make a suicide look like a murder—?" Windy halted abruptly. Sat straight up. "Oh my God—!"

"What?"

"Dr. Wells—he found her. Probably with the gun in her hand. He obviously knows she committed suicide."

I blew out a breath, long and slow. "Can't you imagine," I said, "how big of a failure he'd appear to be in everyone's eyes if his daughter committed suicide because she couldn't stand to live with him any longer?"

"Like she chose death rather than life with her father." Windy dragged her hand through her spiky hair. "Jesus...what a thought."

"Death was the easiest alternative she could find."

"Maybe she thought it was the *only* alternative."

"We've got to find out," I said, "if it really was a suicide."

"How?"

I twisted my glass around and around on the tabletop, leaving wet rings.

"I don't know for sure," I said. "But I think that's the only way I can save myself."

Seventeen

It was six o'clock when I halted my pickup in the drive next to my folks' farmhouse and killed the motor. The sun was starting to drop in the blue sky. Mom and Dad would be less than delighted with me. I'd walked out on breakfast, and I'd missed supper. And chores.

They'd be wondering where I'd gone, what I was doing to climb out of the cesspool I'd tumbled into, how I was going to stop myself from drowning.

They sat at the picnic table under the willow tree in the back of the house, both on the same side, and watched me closely as I stepped out of the pickup. A pitcher of lemonade with ice cubes in it sweated on the picnic table. Two tall glasses sat on the table, one in front of Dad, the other in front of Mom, both half-full. Turned upside down, a third glass sat on the table.

Mallard bounded out of the bed of the pickup and ran to Mom and Dad, wagging his tail. Obviously, my folks had been waiting for me. They'd never done this before, wait for me outside on the picnic table.

"Hi," I said sheepishly, expecting an immediate chewing out.

"We were worried about you," Mom said. "Lemonade? Just squeezed."

Their faces looked drawn. For the first time in my life I thought they looked a little old, shadows under their eyes from lack of sleep, Dad a little grayer, Mom's blue eyes troubled. I'd never seen them look like that before, not even a few years ago when they'd had trouble paying their bank loans and thought they might lose the farm. I'd filled their lives with so much sudden and unexpected trauma they were aging right in front of my eyes. *Nice job, Billy. You asshole.*

"Sit down," Dad said.

I sat across from him.

"Called Windy's," he said. "Hans said you and her went fishing."

"Went to the Atalissa quarry for a while, just to get away and try to figure things out."

"What's she say about all this?" Mom said.

"She's…ticked at me."

"Don't blame her," Dad said. "So are we."

"Umm…we went to see Eric Benson and Dr. Wells."

"Eric Benson?" Mom poured a glass full of lemonade and handed it to me. "Who's that?"

I explained that Eric had been Lisa's boyfriend. "I thought he might know something about her death."

I decided I wasn't going to mention my suicide theory until I had some kind of proof. A note, maybe.

I took a deep swallow of the cold, slightly sour lemonade and shivered.

Mom said, "She had a boyfriend while you carried on with her?"

"Actually, they weren't all that close."

"You think he killed her?" Dad said.

I shrugged. "I don't know. He could've, but I'm not sure what his motive might've been. Um…I've got something I want to check in the house."

"What did Dr. Wells say?" Dad said.

"I'll be right back." I set my glass of lemonade on the picnic table. "Mallard's hungry; I'll get his food."

"We want to talk to you," Mom said. "Don't run off."

"I'll be right back."

I hurried into the house and down the basement steps to my room, snapping on the ceiling light. I whipped open my closet door. I dug in the corner on the floor until I found the jeans I'd worn when I visited Lisa last night.

If she'd committed suicide, it was reasonable to assume she might have left me a note.

Heart hammering, I plopped down on the bed, jeans in hand. She might have stuffed a note into one of my jeans pockets, knowing I'd find it later. I ripped the front pockets inside out, spilling change, gum wrappers, and a piece of hard candy onto the bed.

No note.

I dug in the back pockets. I poked two fingers into the watch pocket.

No note.

I fell back on my bed and glanced at the ceiling. The stupid cop who searched for guns in the rafters hadn't put the tiles back straight.

Then I sat up and smiled at my own foolishness.

If Lisa had written me a note, she wouldn't have put it in my jeans. I might have found it last night when I got home and called the police or her father, stopping her.

She might have left a note in my locker at school, though.

I hadn't gone to my locker Friday after school because I'd been in a hurry to get out for the holiday. I'd hauled everything I needed to study over the weekend with me to seventh period study hall. After the last bell, I'd dashed out the door, straight for my pickup.

My locker, that's where she'd always left notes before, slipped in through the air vents. She might have delivered one after school, after she was sure I'd gone home for the weekend. That way she'd know I wouldn't find it until after she'd killed herself.

I swore under my breath.

Because of the holiday, I couldn't get into school until Tuesday. I'd go crazy waiting.

I fetched the bag of liver-flavored dry dog food from under the kitchen sink. The kitchen smelled of fried pork chops, one of my favorites, but I wasn't hungry. I went outside, filled the dog's bowl by the back door, whistled, and Mallard came running. I set the bag of food inside the door.

Tuesday!

Definitely too long to wait.

Could I break into the school tonight to search my locker?

"Sit down, Billy," Dad said.

I remained standing at the end of the picnic table, too nervous and edgy to sit now, and reached for my glass of lemonade.

The breeze had stopped blowing and though we were in the shade of the willow tree, the air suddenly felt hot and humid. I took another deep swallow of lemonade.

"We still have leftover chicken," Mom said, "if you're hungry. Ate all the pork chops. Didn't make you any. Didn't know if you'd be here or not."

"It's all right," I said. "Windy and I ate at the Tastee-Freez."

"What did Dr. Wells say?" Dad said. "I'm surprised he talked to you."

I set my glass on the table and stuffed my hands into my jeans pockets.

"Weren't you afraid to go there?" Mom said.

"Yes, but Windy and I wanted to find out about his stepson. He's another person who might be involved in this. And I tried to convince Dr. Wells I didn't kill his daughter."

"Did he believe you?" Mom said.

"Not hardly. The gun the cops found in my pickup was his."

"His?" Dad said.

I nodded. "And he says he's going to make sure I hang for Lisa's death."

"Oh my," Mom said, her hand fluttering to her throat.

"Now that Moody knows where the gun came from," I said, "he's going to be more convinced than ever I killed Lisa. What's with him?"

Mom and Dad exchanged a swift glance.

Dad shook his head, but Mom said, "Yes, Will, we're going to tell him…"

"Some things are better left alone," Dad said.

"I want him to know we understand," Mom said. "Sit down, Billy. Please."

I rubbed my neck, feeling the tension in my muscles, and finally sat on the edge of the seat across from Mom.

"This is your mother's idea," Dad said, "telling you this."

"He doesn't want me speaking," Mom said, "because he doesn't want you thinking badly of us." Mom wrung her hands. "As a girl, ever since I could remember, sixth grade or so, I was Henry Moody's girlfriend."

I blinked. Was she kidding? *That creep?* I couldn't believe it, but I didn't say anything.

"Your grandpa was the banker in Clear Creek. Henry's father was the town's mayor." Mom smiled at Dad. "Your father went to high school with us."

"A farm boy," Dad said. "Like you, Billy."

Mom smiled. "I would catch him looking at me lots of times, though I didn't pay him much attention."

Dad laced his thick fingers.

"Were you and Moody friends?" I asked him.

"We got to be," Dad said. "He was friendly with me because I knew places to take him hunting and fishing. We spent some time together."

Mom went on. "During July every summer, lots of high school kids detasseled corn. It was maybe ten days work, sometimes two weeks, like now, and the wages were good. Henry never detasseled, but I did because my father thought it was good I earn my own money and learn to save."

"I worked to put clothes on my back," Dad said.

"Detasseling corn," Mom said, blushing, "that's when we got acquainted."

The thought of my folks as teenagers sneaking off into

a cornfield to make out brought a grin to my face. No wonder Moody was pissed at Dad.

"Of course we never did nothing"—Mom struggled for the right words—"nothing like young people do now."

What she wanted to say was *Like you've been doing, Billy, with Lisa Wells. Night after night.*

"I understand, Mom."

"Eileen," Dad said, "why don't you drop it?"

Mom waved him off with a flap of her hand. "After graduation, your father and me got real serious. Secretly, of course."

Like Lisa and me!

Dad said, "I don't want you to talk about it anymore."

"Will, let me finish—"

"No," Dad said quietly. "That's enough."

Mom poured more lemonade for herself. She remained silent, her forehead wrinkled, her cheeks still a little red. I waited for her to defy Dad and to continue.

Dad stared at his laced fingers resting on the table.

But suddenly, though I was dying to hear the rest of the story, I decided I didn't want Mom to get into deeper trouble with Dad by urging her to tell me more. I knew she'd tell me the rest of the story eventually—I just knew it. I'd wait.

So I said, "Well, Moody can't get even with you guys. I didn't kill Lisa or steal her dad's guns." I gulped the last of my lemonade, emptying the glass. "And I'm going to prove it to Cedar County Sheriff Henry Moody myself."

"How?" Mom said.

"I don't know exactly, but I will."

"If need be," Dad said, "we'll get a lawyer. Don't you talk to him again without one."

"They cost too much," I said.

"What needs to be," Mom said, "will be."

"We'll borrow against the farm," Dad said.

"I won't let you," I said. "If it comes to that, I'll get a public defender."

Dad shook his head.

"No you won't," Mom said. "And that's final. You're more important than this farm."

I felt choked.

My folks were telling me they'd risk the farm—their Century Farm—for lawyer fees to save my sorry ass, even though I'd humiliated them and destroyed their faith in me, even though they hated what I'd done with Lisa and the evidence seemed to indicate I'd robbed her dad and killed her.

My parents deserved a better son than me.

Eighteen

That night I lay on my back in bed staring at the darkened ceiling. The bedroom was cool, yet I lay in my underwear without a sheet or blanket. Mallard dozed on his throw rug beside the bed. I lowered my arm to scratch the dog's ribs. He groaned, and his hind leg beat helplessly on the floor.

What a story my folks had to tell. Even though I didn't know all of it, I knew the ending: Mom dumped her childhood sweetheart to marry the man she loved. Why couldn't Lisa have defied her dad like that for me?

Our bond wasn't strong enough, that's why. Our love wasn't true love. Not like the love Mom and Dad had for each other. How do you know if what you're feeling is love? Or if your love will last? Somehow, love comes first, then lovemaking. That's how it's supposed to work, I think. "Horse before the cart," Dad always says.

What Lisa and I experienced might have become love, though, if we'd had more time. If we'd become friends. Close friends.

I shook my head. I didn't know when I'd ever get my brain to think straight again.

A little after 10:00 PM., I crept up the basement stairs, opened the kitchen door softly—I commanded Mallard to go back down—and quietly lifted the wall phone from the hook. I hoped to get a cell phone for graduation so I wouldn't have to sneak around like this to make private phone calls all the time.

I didn't turn on the kitchen light. A beam from the pole-top yard light outside lit the kitchen with a pale glow, and the smell of fried pork chops lingered.

As I shuffled over to the fridge, pulling the coiled phone cord with me, I punched in Windy's number. I opened the fridge door. The light popped on. I found the leftover chicken wrapped in aluminum foil in the meat keeper.

"What do you want?" Windy said, and yawned when she answered the phone and heard my voice.

I sat at the kitchen table, the phone-shoulder hugged to my ear. I unwrapped the chicken: two thighs, a breast, and a wing. Great.

I said, "You think Ms. Jameison could get me into school tomorrow morning? She's a coach. She's got keys."

"Why?"

"So I can look in my locker. See if Lisa left me a suicide note."

"Wait till Tuesday."

"I'll go crazy. If Moody comes around here tomorrow and tries to haul me off to jail, I want something to throw in his face, something so I can say, 'Here! Read this suicide note! Lisa shot herself. What do you think of that?'"

"You'll have to explain to Ms. Jameison why you want in the school building, and she'll probably think you *are* crazy."

"Lisa's giving things away follows a pattern. It means something."

"I'm not sure teachers are authorized to go into the building when it's locked for holidays. She'd probably have to call the principal or something."

"Are you sure?"

"Wait till Tuesday. If there's a note in your locker, it's not going anywhere."

I bit off a chunk of chicken thigh and thought about that. I reached across the table for salt and pepper.

"Does the school have a nighttime security system?"

Windy didn't answer.

"Hey, you still there?"

"Billy O'Reilly! Of course there's a security system. If you break into that school, bells will ring, sirens will wail, lights will flash, and you'll be videotaped. The cops will be there in five seconds to throw your stupid ass in jail for sure!"

"Don't get excited, I was just asking."

"I've got a better idea."

"What?"

"Promise me you won't break into school."

"I promise."

"I mean it, Billy."

"What's your idea?"

"Listen," Windy said, "we get to school Tuesday morning early. Five-forty-five or earlier. Mary Alice works in the attendance office before and after school. All the students' schedule cards are on file in the office. First thing in the morning she's by herself."

"So?"

"Think about it," Windy said. "The schedule cards have your locker number on them and lock combination numbers."

"Will she get Lisa's combination for us?"

"I can talk her into it, I know I can."

"I hate to wait."

"Listen to me. Tuesday morning, you check your locker while I get Lisa's combination numbers. If you don't find a note, we clear out Lisa's locker before her counselor, the principal, or anybody else does. We might find something in *her* locker about suicide."

"You're right."

"Maybe she kept a journal."

I polished off the chicken thigh, set the bone on the aluminum foil, and reached for the breast.

"You're brilliant," I said.

"I want you to repeat after me: I will not break into school tonight."

I swallowed a bite and cleared my throat. I needed a cold glass of milk. "I will not break into school tonight."

"You mean it?"

"Yes."

"Promise?"

"You don't trust me?"

"Stupid question after what you've been doing, Billy. Good night."

"Are you still pissed at me?"

"I told you, for the rest of my life."

"Why are you helping me?"

She hung up.

When I stood and reached to hang up the phone, the lights in the kitchen flashed on, and I nearly jumped out of my skin.

Dad was looming in the doorway, dressed in only his boxer shorts, his massive chest thick with gray-black curly hair.

I blinked in the sudden bright light, then tried to smile. "I was hungry, and I needed to call Windy."

"Break into what school tonight?" Dad crossed his

arms and leaned against the doorjamb. I hung up the phone and sat back down at the kitchen table.

"You were listening?" I said.

"Mom heard a noise in the kitchen. I came down. Me and your Mom couldn't get to sleep, knowing you've been sneaking out at night."

I felt my face flush. "Dad, I'm not going to break into any school. Windy and I were just talking. It was nothing, really."

Dad frowned at me.

"Honest, Dad. I'm not breaking into school."

"Make sure you clean the table before you go back to bed."

"I will. I need a glass of milk."

Dad watched me as I got up and opened the fridge door. I wondered if he was going to watch while I poured the milk and drank it, making sure I went down to bed.

"One other thing," he said, and sighed. "I might as well finish that little story your mom was telling you earlier, so's she won't have to."

"Dad, it's really none of my business." I sat down again, glass of milk in hand.

"Might help you understand more about Moody, I admit that." Dad shifted his weight. Looked at the floor. Then at me. "Your mom and Moody had become engaged."

My head snapped up. "She was actually going to marry him? I can't believe it."

"Lots of pressure from his folks. And hers."

"Still…"

"The date was all set." Dad cleared his throat. "What happened was me and some of Henry's other buddies threw him a bachelor party on the Friday night before he and your mom were to be married on Saturday. Party was at a tavern in Durant, the Do Drop Inn—it's torn down now. I was to be his best man."

"Oh, wow!"

"About ten AM I claimed I was sick—drank too much. So I faked staggering out. I picked your mom up at the Clear Creek movie house where she was waiting for me."

"You and Mom obviously had this planned?"

Mom suddenly appeared next to Dad in the doorway, wrapped in her pink robe, her hair all tousled.

"We did," she said.

Dad looked down at her, frowning again. "Well, you might as well finish it. Seems you're bound to."

"Your dad picked me up at the theater," Mom said, "and we drove around. Parked. Your dad had been drinking—"

"That had nothing to do with it," he said.

"We had never done anything like that before," Mom said. "Least I hadn't."

She looked up at Dad, but he didn't say a word.

"I wanted it to be that way," Mom said. "With your father, the first time."

I sat in silence, amazed at what my mom was admitting to me, she and Dad sneaking around behind Moody's back. Hooking up for the first time the night before she was to marry another man. Dad and Mom had gotten carried away, too, just like Lisa and me.

How did they know it was love?

"What happened?" I said. "Someone told Moody?"

Mom slipped her arm around Dad's waist. "We promised ourselves not to tell, but I called Henry the next morning, early, and told him what we'd done, your dad and me. Told him I could never love anyone else. Could never be happy with him."

"Oh, wow!" I said again.

"He came looking for me," Dad said. "We fought. I beat the hell out of him right in the drive out there." Dad almost smiled at the memory. "And that was the end of it."

"Except," Mom said, "when the wedding was called off so sudden like that it was a terrible scandal for everyone. Soon the whole county knew."

"I'll bet," I said.

"Moody lost face," Mom said. "Your dad and me felt terrible for him, and we were embarrassed nearly to death. All the gifts had to be returned."

"Now," Dad said, "he thinks he's got a chance to get even."

"He's mistaken," I said.

"But you see how he feels he's got just cause," Mom said.

"I understand."

"Sorry," Dad said.

"*Sorry!*" I said. "I'm the one who's sorry. None of us would be in the situation if it weren't for me."

Mom rubbed her eyes, and Dad said, "Goodnight."

"Night."

"Clean up your mess," Mom said. "Night."

"Night."

As I cleared off the table, I told myself again I hadn't stolen anything, hadn't killed anyone—I was safe. I wouldn't need a lawyer. My folks wouldn't have to risk the farm for me. But all the while I wondered if Moody was a clever enough cop, hateful enough person to really stick me.

He certainly had his reasons.

I opened the kitchen door and crept back down the stairs to my basement bedroom. Mallard jumped on me, whining. I petted him and then flopped stomach first on my bed in the dark.

A weird thought slipped into my brain, a thought that unnerved me a little. Gave me a little chill. I had done the same thing to Eric that Dad had done to Moody: steal his woman.

I wondered how Moody must have felt after Mom told him what Dad and she had done. He must have been ass-kicking pissed, I'll bet. Then Dad beats him up. At that point, I'll bet he hated Dad enough to kill him. But he didn't because he had a law man's mentality; he understood the consequences of his actions. And now Moody had aimed his sights at me. He could get even with Dad by sending me to jail. He could get even with Dad legally.

Right now, Moody must've been feeling himself in the grip of an all-time high. Like he'd climbed to the top of the world.

I rolled over onto my back. My hand slipped to the side of the bed and I reached down to scratch Mallard's forehead.

Eric must hate me as much as Moody hated Dad. I couldn't blame Eric, I guess. I could almost feel sorry for him. Almost.

Then another disturbing thought invaded my brain. I wondered if Eric and I were going to be lifelong enemies like Dad and Moody? After he graduated from law school, Eric planned to return to State Center. He might become a county prosecutor someday, and maybe someday he'd have a chance to put my son—if I ever married and had kids—behind bars. The Bensons and the O'Reillys—had Eric and I started a feud? Like Dad and Moody?

I hoped not. That was no way to live.

I don't think I fell asleep until two or three in the morning.

Nineteen

I woke Monday morning—Memorial Day—at dawn, only hours after I'd fallen asleep, and prayed Lisa's death and my involvement had all been a silly dream. I knew it wasn't a dream, though, so I promised myself I was going to go through the day pretending nothing had happened, everything was normal. For a day I'd force the tragedy out of my mind. I'd do chores, help Dad with whatever, have breakfast, then study for my semester evaluations.

No Memorial Day picnics for me. No TV or radio. I didn't want to hear any news. I'd gotten enough news yesterday. All of it bad.

I'd decide later about calling Windy.

Maybe Mallard and I would take a walk alone in the woods.

At breakfast, Mom, Dad, and I talked about how well the corn was doing. Could use a little more rain now. It was in the forecast for tomorrow. But today would be a sunny day for all the Memorial Day ceremonies. That was good.

Really, my folks seemed to be pretending right along with me that nothing had happened. They didn't mention Lisa or what I'd done.

It wasn't until after breakfast that Dad went out to the mailbox by the road and came back with the newspaper that my day fell apart.

At the kitchen table, Dad scanned the front page, then held the front section out for me.

"You might want to look at this," he said.

Mom glanced at the paper. "Maybe not, Billy."

At that instant, pretending nothing had happened evaporated.

I grabbed the section and took it into the front room where I could read it by myself. I slumped down on the edge of the sofa, and the second I looked at the paper, I felt as if a mule had kicked me in the chest.

Headlines across the top of the paged screamed: LISA WELLS MURDERED. Splashed across the page in color, Lisa's graduation picture revealed how beautiful she was—long blond hair, blue eyes, thin nose, full lips, strong chin.

As I held the trembling page, tears rushed to my eyes,

and I could hardly read the story, which didn't reveal anything that I didn't already know. I was glad to see my name wasn't mentioned anywhere, but words like "tragic," "ironic," and "despicable" kept cropping up in the story. When I came to a quote from Sheriff Moody, I stabbed the tears out of my eyes so I could see better: "It was a vicious, cowardly crime committed by someone the victim knew very well. We have several strong pieces of evidence, some very clear leads, and a likely suspect. We expect to make an arrest shortly."

"Says you," I muttered.

The story's final paragraph said arrangements were pending for the visitation and the funeral. The visitation would be private.

I flung the paper on the floor.

———

That afternoon, the sun high and hot in another blue, cloudless sky, I took Mallard for a walk down to the creek in the woods on the far side of Dad's cornfield. Mom and Dad had gone to the cemetery to pay their respects to our kinfolk. I didn't go. I didn't want to meet people, listen to their gossip, and maybe have to answer questions from the ones with inquiring minds.

"Did you know the Wells girl very well, Billy?"

"I understand her father simply adored her. Is that true?"

"I think one of her classmates killed her. What do you think, Billy?"

Mallard jumped, splashed, and swam in the creek,

and I sat in the cool shade under a hickory tree, throwing stones into the water.

Earlier, I'd tried studying chemistry in my room, but my effort was pointless. Lisa kept invading my mind. Everything seemed so pointless: breathing, talking, studying. I realized my whole life would be pointless until I knew exactly what had happened to her.

I mean, I'd dated other girls before her. Nobody steady. But all through high school, I'd made out okay at dances and after football, basketball, and volleyball games. Once last year, at Melanie Harper's Halloween farmyard bonfire, I almost did it with her in her dad's barn, which would have been my first time. But I got too excited. I blew it. Literally. She thought that was funny, sort of chuckled, and I was so embarrassed I walked out. Later, I saw her strolling toward the barn in the moonlight with Brian Walker. Melanie and I never tried to hook up again. I was too humiliated to face her, and she probably thought I wasn't worth the effort.

Lisa was my first time.

She kept me cool and called me "sweetie." I didn't panic, and everything worked out better than I could have imagined or planned. Nobody had ever looked at me the way Lisa had. Touched me the way she had. And I seemed to thrill her, too. That first night she was like, "God! I love the feel of you inside me!" I mean, I thought I'd die, Lisa Wells telling me stuff like that.

My moments with her had been so new, fresh, and

thrilling I knew they would remain in my brain forever, clear as snapshots.

And now she was gone.

Was it love? I wondered again. *Or just sex?*

Maybe it was more than *just* sex. Maybe it was the thrill of discovery.

I hurled a stone into the creek.

Guilt splashed over me.

Why hadn't the little things she'd said and done beforehand tipped me off to her thoughts of suicide? If I'd been smarter, I could have stopped her. I could have saved her.

———————

I was walking home with Mallard, my boots crunching on the gravel road, only a quarter mile away from the house, when I heard the car racing up behind me.

Instinctively, I knew it was Moody.

I turned to look. The blue and white cruiser bore down on me like a heat-seeking missile.

I called Mallard to my side at the edge of the road, commanding the dog to sit.

The car shot past us, then skidded to a halt, leaving Mallard and me fighting a whirling dust cloud.

Moody opened the door and stepped out of the cruiser, a taunting smile twisting his lips.

"Nice day for a boy and his dog to take a walk," he said, and strolled toward us. "I was coming by to talk to you. Didn't recognize you at first. Sorry about the dust."

"It's always dusty here. Too expensive to oil the road."

"Where you been?"

I poked my hands into the back pockets of my jeans. "Walking."

"Been in the woods behind your daddy's place?"

"Might've been."

"Know them woods pretty good, do you?"

"I hunt there."

"I used to hunt there with your daddy years ago. Good place to hide guns. Wrap 'em up all tight in plastic. Dig a hole. Cover 'em with dirt and leaves."

Mallard whined, and I waved him off to prowl in the weedy ditch. Maybe he'd flush a pheasant—he loved that.

"About a hundred acres of woods there," I said, allowing myself a faint smile. "Why don't you go look for the guns? See what you find. See how long it takes you. I'll talk to you again next year. After you've given up."

"Sometimes you got a smart mouth, Billy-boy. That's not good for a lad in your fix. Dr. Wells says you were at his house yesterday, harassing him."

"I wasn't harassing him."

"Says you wanted to walk right in his house and look around."

"I wanted to tell him I was sorry for what I'd done, sneaking into his house and sleeping with Lisa, but I didn't kill her. Didn't steal anything."

"Dr. Wells's got enough problems. I'll make this short:

Stay away from his place. I don't want to hear you're caus-
ing him more problems. Or me. Hear?"

"I'm not your problem."

Moody pursed his lips beneath his thin mustache. "The
gun we found in your jeep was the murder weapon. Did I
tell you that?"

My stomach lurched. "Find my fingerprints on it?"

"No prints at all. But it's not uncommon for a gun
lover like you to wipe a piece clean after he's handled it.
Natural thing to do. Wipe it off."

"I never touched that gun."

"A twenty-five automatic doesn't make much of a hole.
But it's deadly when pointed right at a victim's heart."

"Is that where Lisa was shot, the heart?"

Moody gazed up at the blue sky, squinting and shad-
ing his eyes with his hand. "Is that a question to make you
sound innocent? Like you don't know what happened?"

"Was she shot in the heart?"

"Close range."

I looked down at the gravel and kicked at the stones.
Mallard still prowled the tall grass in the ditch.

I shuddered at the thought of Lisa's pointing the gun
directly at her heart, probably holding it with both hands,
then closing her eyes, and squeezing the trigger. God, what
was she thinking? *There's no other way. No other choice.*

I licked my lips. "I know why you want to pin this on
me."

"Pin it on you?"

"My mom and dad finally told me."

Moody smiled. "Your daddy tell you how he betrayed me, did he? How he forced Eileen to betray me and herself?"

"They loved each other. Mom was honest with you. Give her credit for that."

Moody wagged a steely finger in my face. "What happened twenty years ago between me and your folks has nothing to do with what's going on right here and now."

"I don't believe it."

"I'm out to catch a killer and send a message: no more kids killing kids in my county."

"Isn't it possible Lisa committed suicide?" I said. "She could've held the gun with both hands and aimed at her heart. She probably knew where her dad kept it."

"Suicide gets you off the hook, doesn't it?"

"It's the only logical answer."

"But the notion leaves big questions. First thing is why does a brilliant, beautiful girl like Lisa Wells, with everything going for her—so loved by her daddy—kill herself?"

"She didn't have everything going for her."

"She had looks, money, brains, talent—a daddy who loved her. Ain't much more."

"She was giving some of her valuables away—I'm telling you she killed herself."

Moody shook his head. "Second thing is we ran tests on both her hands. Negative. She hadn't fired a gun."

I kicked at the gravel road again.

"And third, the gun was found in *your* pickup—"

"Because someone dumped it there."

"Not found beside her. Not found in her hand. But in *your* pickup truck."

"Ask Dr. Wells if she committed suicide. He knows, he found her. See if he freaks. Watch him crumble."

"Another thing," Moody said. "Ninety-nine percent of suicides shoot themselves in the temple or through the roof of their mouth. Not through the heart. Too awkward."

"Lisa shot herself in the heart because that's where she hurt most."

"Not likely." Moody fingered his mustache. "You're going to jail, Billy-boy. And you stay away from Dr. Wells's place, or it'll be sooner than you think. Get a lawyer."

Moody climbed into his cruiser, started it, slammed it into gear, and sped away. The car's tires hurled stones at me and created another dust storm.

As I started home again, scuffing at the gravel with my boots, Mallard scrambled out of to the weeds in the ditch to trot alongside me.

Neither of Lisa's hands had borne traces of gunpowder. She hadn't fired a weapon.

How could that be?

Dr. Wells had cleaned her hands off.

He knew about guns and gunpowder residue.

I prayed my locker or Lisa's provided a real answer to this mystery.

Twenty

On Tuesday morning, in the silent, dimly lit halls of State Center High School at 6:05 AM, I stood in front of my open locker, staring inside in disbelief.

No note from Lisa had tumbled out.

They always tumbled out and fluttered to the floor. They always got stuck between the door and all the junk I had crammed in there.

I opened the door, and they always fluttered out.

But not this morning.

I pawed on the top shelf among pencils, pens, chewing gum, an empty pop can, an overdue paperback from the school library, and a month-old copy of the school newspaper.

No note.

I always lined my books upright on the bottom of the locker, then piled my other stuff on top of them: gym bag, extra pair of Nikes, a grubby sweatshirt that had slipped off the hook in back. Stuff like that. I ripped through all that junk, knowing I was wasting time.

Lisa's notes always fluttered out. But not this time.

I stuffed my backpack into my locker.

Cussing, I slammed the locker door shut and smacked it with the heel of my doubled fist.

Windy would be waiting for me in front of Lisa's locker with the lock combination, if Mary Alice would give it to her. Early-bird classes started at 6:45 AM. Windy and I had to get in and out of Lisa's locker before a single person came strolling by this morning and became suspicious.

———————

On the second floor, near the Instructional Media Center—the library—I twisted the dial on Lisa's combination lock and yanked.

Stuck!

I yanked the lock again.

"What's wrong?" Windy set her backpack beside her on the floor.

"It won't open." I yanked once more, gritting my teeth. "You sure Mary Alice gave you the right numbers?"

"Yes!"

"Read them again."

Windy looked at the slip of paper in the palm of her hand and read: "Right, thirty-two. Left, twenty-nine. Two turns right, fifteen."

"I thought you said the last number was thirteen."

"*Fifteen!* C'mon, Billy. We haven't got all day."

I glanced at my watch. Six-twenty. We'd be dead if Edwards, the librarian, came swinging around the corner, and nabbed us cleaning out Lisa's locker.

He opened the library at 6:30 AM.

I spun the dial again, worked it through the numbers, and yanked. "Got it!" I pulled the lock off, unlatched the locker, and swung the door open.

The lavender scent inside Lisa's locker rocked me.

"What's wrong?" Windy said.

"Nothing."

All her gear was carefully arranged. She was such a neat freak.

I said, "Get her notebooks and folders from the bottom. I'll get the stuff from the top."

Windy bent and cleared the bottom of the locker, where Lisa had set her texts upright, notebooks and folders squeezed in between them. Windy crammed everything into her backpack.

Brushing aside a hair spray can, hand lotion bottle, lipstick tube, and hairbrush, I grabbed three folders lying flat on the top shelf. Lisa's blue and gold letterman's jacket hung on a hook. Maybe she'd written a suicide note, stuffed it into her jacket pocket, and had chickened out about delivering it to me.

I dug in the pockets. Nothing in the first. What I dragged out of the second startled me worse than her scent had. I stepped back as I turned a Ziplock bag over in my hand, eyeballing the contents that looked like dried, cut weeds.

Jesus Christ!

"C'mon!" Windy slung her backpack onto her shoulders. "Close the door. We got to get out of here."

I jammed the plastic bag into my jeans pocket—quick so Windy couldn't see it. I'd show her later. We needed to haul ass. *Now!* I slammed the door shut, replaced the lock, and spun the dial.

Fifteen feet away from us, Eric Benson came striding around the corner. When he spotted us standing in front of Lisa's locker, he stopped dead in his tracks, his jaw dropping. "What the hell are you guys doing here?"

I stood paralyzed, couldn't even think, but I'll give Windy credit. She said calmly, "Waiting for the library to open up."

"That's bullshit!" he said, and marched toward us. "You're trying to break into Lisa's locker."

"Why would we?" Windy said. "She doesn't have anything we want."

He eyed Windy's bulging backpack. "Shit! You already

broke into her locker—what did you find?" Eric's eyes looked massive behind his glasses.

My voice finally returned. "You're crazy. We don't know her combination. We couldn't break in if we wanted to."

"I want every damn thing you found," Eric said.

"What are you *afraid* we found?" Windy said.

"I want it *now!*" He started to reach for Windy. I imagined he was going to rip her backpack off her shoulders. I caught him by surprise. I butted him up against the lockers with my chest—his head banged off a locker door—and I snarled at him: "We weren't in her locker!"

"The hell you weren't!"

"Uh-oh!" Windy said.

At that instant, Mr. Edwards came waltzing up to us, an umbrella and attaché case in hand—I hadn't seen him approaching.

He looked at Eric and me, "What's going on, gentlemen?"

"Nothing," Windy said.

"Nothing," I said. I backed off of Eric. "We're just leaving."

"These guys were trying to break into that locker," Eric said, and pointed at Lisa's locker door.

"Not so," Windy said.

I grabbed her hand, and we fled down the hallway, leaving Eric flatfooted. I'm sure he wanted to chase us. But he couldn't. He was in a bind. He had to stay there until after Mr. Edwards opened the library and went inside. Eric had to search Lisa's locker to see if anything was missing.

Like marijuana.

————————

At 6:45 AM, Windy and I sat hunched in my pickup, parked eight blocks from school in the nearly empty State Center Municipal Parking Lot. We poured over the notebooks and folders we'd escaped with.

The morning had dawned cool and cloudy, a gray sky threatening rain, just as the weatherman had forecasted.

I hadn't told Windy what I'd found. I hated to make Lisa look even worse in Windy's eyes. But I'd have to tell Windy sooner or later. I still couldn't believe what I'd found.

Lisa was smoking pot.

"Nothing here about suicide." Windy leafed through a green notebook on her lap. "Nothing but history notes." She snapped the notebook closed. "I keep wondering why Eric was so shook. What did he think we were going to find?"

I ignored Windy's question. "Nothing here, either." I flipped through the pages of Lisa's American lit journal. I felt guilty reading her private thoughts about the lit selections she'd read. All of the entries were written in black ink in her oval hand. Jameison had scribbled comments in red ink in the margins: "Excellent!" "Well written!" "Good insight!"

"It's almost seven-twenty," Windy said. "We've got to get to school."

Regular classes started at 7:45 AM.

"Have we looked at everything?" I said.

"I think so. I can't believe how methodical she is…" Windy's eyes met mine. "*Was*…I'm sorry."

I looked at the floor by Windy's feet where we'd lain each item as we'd finished with it. Lisa had five classes and she had kept a different colored notebook for each one. For each class she also kept a pocket folder in which she saved daily assignments, quizzes, and tests that had been returned. She'd carefully filed the papers in each folder according to the due dates. The colors of the notebooks and folders matched each other. For three classes she'd kept journals: American lit, World Cultures, and French V. The French journal was written in French. Neither Windy nor I could translate it. We'd taken Spanish.

Windy said, "She was talented and smart, I'll give her that. It's hard to believe she committed suicide."

"Or was maybe smoking up." I dug the plastic bag I'd taken from Lisa's jacket out of my pocket and held it up.

"Holy shit! Where'd you get that?"

"From a pocket in Lisa's letterman's jacket."

"God! No wonder Eric freaked when he thought we'd searched Lisa's locker."

"I can't believe she was smoking pot."

"Maybe they were both potheads. You found their stash."

"I never smelled marijuana on her."

"She always dipped herself in expensive perfume." Windy took the bag from me, shook it, and peered at its contents. "Looks like oregano. Eric had to get it out of her locker before anyone else discovered it."

I thought a moment. "She told me once Eric wasn't good for her, she needed to be away from him—I think I understand why."

Windy tossed the bag to me. "Why would she be smoking?"

"A way to escape, probably. To feel free. To defy her dad."

"Get rid of the stuff, Billy. You can't take it back to school, you can't leave it in your truck."

"It shows you how screwed up she was." I opened the bag, smelled the weed. "I'll dump it in a trash barrel over there in the corner of the lot and burn it—if the barrel's empty. Any matches in the glove compartment?"

Windy opened the compartment and poked around. "Shotgun shells, that's all. Dump the stuff out. Let it blow away."

I held the bag out the pickup door and shook it, releasing the weed into the wind, and a small slip of paper flew out. I climbed out of the truck and picked the paper up before it fluttered away across the blacktop.

"Get rid of the bag, too." Windy said.

I looked at the paper and recognized Lisa's handwriting: "Under the desk an attic door."

Reaching inside the truck, I handed the slip to Windy. "Read this."

I trotted over and threw the plastic bag into the trash barrel. When I climbed back into the truck, Windy said, "What do you suppose it means, 'Under the desk an attic door'? Is it a message to someone?"

"I don't know. There's a desk in her room, but an attic door would be in the ceiling."

"Is there one there?"

"I can't remember."

"Not on your back very often?"

I looked at Windy, my face feeling red, but her brown eyes lowered before they could meet mine.

"Sorry," she said. "That was nasty, I didn't mean that."

I shrugged. "What did you do with the note?"

"I put it in the glove compartment. What are we going to do with all her other things?"

"I'll go through them again at home. Maybe we missed something."

"Nothing in your locker, right? You're positive?"

"Positive."

I felt defeated.

I hadn't found a suicide note in my locker. Hadn't read anything about suicide in Lisa's journals. Neither had Windy.

All I'd discovered was that Lisa was maybe smoking pot.

Under the desk an attic door.

What could it mean?

Who was it written to? Why?

Maybe my suicide theory was wrong. Either Eric or Rodney had killed Lisa, as I'd first suspected. Rodney seemed the more logical choice. But Eric could just as well be the murderer. As well as a drug user. But what was Eric's motivation for killing Lisa?

Then, as if she'd been reading my mind, Windy looked at me and said, "What if Eric whacked himself out on weed that night, then went back to Lisa's house after you left, sneaked into her bedroom just like you had, and told her if he couldn't have her neither could you."

"Like he wanted her to make a choice? He gave her an ultimatum?"

"Right. And maybe she refused to make a choice—she didn't want either one of you."

"She didn't want me, I know that."

"She didn't want Eric—"

"She actually told me she didn't want him."

"—so he shot her—no one else could have her."

"Makes sense," I said.

Then Windy's eyes got big, and I could tell another thought had zipped through her brain.

"He killed her," Windy said, "and intended to kill himself—a murder and a suicide. But he chickened out."

I shook my head. "I don't know—that seems a little too far over the top."

"Desperate lovers do that all the time—murder, then suicide! Remember, he's fucked up."

"How did he get Dr. Wells's gun to kill her?"

"She already had it in her room. Remember, she was going to commit suicide."

"But Eric killed her before she could use it on herself."

"Exactly," Windy said.

"But she was found dead in the living room. Not in her bedroom."

"Eric chased her through the house."

"But Dr. Wells would have awakened and would have stopped Eric. Or at least he would've seen Eric in the house. There'd be no need to frame me."

That stopped Windy. She gave a huge shrug. "You're right, you're absolutely right."

I threw my head back on the seat and rubbed my forehead. Instead of solving anything, Windy and I had just created more confusion.

My own brain seemed ready to explode.

At school, Windy hurried off to her first-period physics class while I stopped at my locker to root around again, hoping I'd find a suicide note. No luck.

I kicked the locker closed, clicked the lock shut, and turned to join the herd of students stampeding to class, but found my path blocked.

Eric Benson stood in my way. Fuming. Red-faced. He poked at his glasses. Adjusted them on his nose. "You took Lisa's notebooks—and what else?" His hands balled into fists.

"We threw your stash away. No one's going to rat you out."

"All of it?"

"All of it. Blown away in the wind."

He looked stricken. "It was some good shit…cost a mint."

"Tough."

"Like you didn't know what she was doing. Like you weren't getting your kicks, too. Everyone experiments."

"Not everyone. How long had she been smoking?"

"Just this spring—long enough to know she liked getting high."

I decided to shoot him out of the sky, just like a clay bird. Turn him to dust. Even if my accusation didn't make sense. See if I could get him to admit to something. *Anything!* "You showed up at her house the night she died—"

"I did not!"

"She told you to get the hell out—she didn't want you. You killed her—no one else could have her."

Eric jumped back from me, his eyes bulging behind his glasses. I couldn't tell if I'd somehow nailed him with the truth or if he thought he was talking to a mad man.

"Your brain was so fried," I said "You didn't know what you were doing. You shot her!"

He laughed at me. He whipped off his glasses and laughed at me. "You're crazy, man. You been smokin' some bad shit."

"I'm not crazy and I don't smoke—I just figured out the truth."

"I was home, I can prove it. My folks don't lie for me."

"You sneaked out. I know you did!"

"I loved her. I'd never hurt her!"

"You *loved* her—so you fed her pot?"

And with that Eric spun around and left me standing alone in the hallway by my locker, gasping for breath, shaking.

As if I'd admitted to shooting Lisa myself.

When I slipped into my Western Civ class at the last second with a lowered head, Dr. Townsend, the school principal, was already making an announcement over the PA to the students.

"...have lost the presence among us of a most beautiful, wonderful, talented girl. At this time I'd like everyone to bow his or her head a minute in silent memory of Lisa Wells, whose tragic death has wrenched all our hearts."

As I slid silently into my seat, twenty-seven student heads dropped over desks. Behind me, Rachel Johnson sniffled. Across from me, Howie Ashford made the sign of the cross. Tom Ward blew his nose. I glanced toward the front of the room. Mr. Smith, our teacher, seemed to be watching me stonily. I wondered if he—like maybe everybody else in school—knew that Lisa had spent part of her last night on earth in bed with me.

I lowered my head and squeezed my eyes shut.

Suddenly ugly thoughts tumbled through my mind like floodwaters over a dyke.

Lisa! Lisa! Did you really kill yourself? Why didn't you leave a note? Did you love me? Don't you think you owed me some kind of explanation? Look at the jam you've gotten me into. I'm accused of your murder. I've been framed. Your dad, Eric, Rodney, Moody—who left the gun in my truck? But you killed yourself, didn't you? Didn't you realize how many people you'd hurt? How much turmoil you'd create? Why were you so selfish? Why didn't you give me a chance to save you? Goddamn, Lisa, why didn't you cut us all a break?

Dr. Townsend's voice crackled again over the loudspeaker: "Thank you very much. At this time I would like to announce that we will be on an early dismissal schedule today. School will end at one-twenty-five so those of you who want to will be able to attend Lisa's funeral at two this afternoon at the United Presbyterian Church in downtown State Center. Following the funeral and burial services, a luncheon will be served in the church basement." Dr. Townsend grabbed a breath. "I would also like to announce that we have several counselors on campus with us this morning who are prepared to present in the Liddy Auditorium a program about grieving. You may also meet with them privately after the assembly, if you wish. Those who are not interested may go to the cafeteria or library for a study hall. The program will take the rest of first period. Your teachers may dismiss you at eight-fifteen. Thank you very much."

I sat hunkered down in a chair at a circular table in the cafeteria study hall. Windy sat across from me. We still had ten minutes to talk quietly before the study hall became silent.

It was never perfectly silent, though.

I'd already told Windy about my visit with Moody yesterday and about his telling me Lisa had been shot in the heart. Windy only shook her head and made a face, like she didn't want to talk about that. The thought was too gross. Now I told her about Eric's catching me by my locker just before classes started.

"So Lisa and Eric *were* getting high together," she said. "Potheads."

"Evidently."

"She was using you for a different kind of high."

I eased my head back and peered at the ceiling for a second. Windy was right; Lisa had been using me all along for her own selfish reasons. She'd manipulated me. The thought hurt. And it hurt even worse as I began to realize how dumb I'd been.

"Why didn't you go to the assembly?" Windy finally said.

"Why'd you follow me to study hall?"

"Because you didn't go to the assembly. Are you going to meet with one of the counselors?"

I shook my head. "I don't want to talk to strangers about Lisa. Talking to Moody has been bad enough. And talking to Eric and Dr. Wells."

"You should see somebody. You look like shit. Are you all right?"

"I'm fine."

"You going to the funeral?"

I nodded. "Maybe Rodney's sobered up, knows about his stepsister's death, and will show up at the funeral this afternoon, perfectly innocent, nothing to hide, but I'd like to talk to him. And I want my seventy-five dollars."

"I'll go with you."

She gave me a look to see if I was going to protest, but why would I? She was my most valuable friend in the world. And she didn't even like me. How ironic was that?

Then I clued Windy in about my mom, dad, and Moody all going to high school together. "Mom and Moody dated in high school. Were even engaged to be married."

"Oh my God! Are you kidding? You mom was engaged to *that* guy?"

"But Dad won out."

I didn't tell Windy the personal stuff about Mom and Dad hooking up the night before she was to marry Moody. I guess out of respect for my folks I decided not to. Let that be their secret.

Windy said, "No wonder Moody doesn't like your dad and wants a piece of you."

"Thinking about Moody and my dad and mom makes me realize *why* Eric hates me. And how much he hates me."

"I was wondering if you'd ever realize how Eric must feel, your sleeping with his girl."

"Took me awhile to figure it out. Now I'm wondering if we'll go on hating each other for the rest of our lives. Like my dad and Moody."

"Eric's got a good enough reason."

I nodded. "Yes, he does."

Windy and I were silent again. Then she ran her hand through her spiky hair. "Where do you suppose the other guns are?"

"If Rodney robbed his dad and killed Lisa, the guns are in the trunk of his car. He'll sell them. He wants the money."

"And if Eric killed her, where are the guns?"

"Not in his house—the cops searched his place."

"Maybe he's got them hidden somewhere and is going to sell them later for drug money."

"Right. Could be."

"If Dr. Wells found Lisa's body," Windy said, "and tried to make a suicide look like a murder and robbery, he must've taken his own guns. What did he do with them? I mean, besides planting one in your truck?"

I sat back in my chair. "I hadn't thought about that. What *did* he do with them?"

"Chances are he didn't hide them in the house. He'd be afraid the cops might find them while looking for other evidence. Maybe he dropped them in the lake."

"He'd want to drop them in the deepest part. He's got a pontoon boat."

"Where else could he hide them?"

I leaned forward, elbows on the table. "When I saw Moody yesterday, he wanted to know if I'd buried the guns in the woods on Dad's place. He asked me if I'd wrapped them in plastic and buried them."

"You think that's what Dr. Wells did?"

"He probably didn't have much time. The nearby woods would be the closest and easiest place to hide something."

"He had to drive to your house, leave the pistol in your truck, then drive back. Bury the guns. Call the police. Not much time at all."

"He's a gun lover," I said. "A true gun lover never wants to part with them. If he dropped them in the lake, they'd rust away. If he buried them in the woods, he could protect them by wrapping them in plastic."

"Then someday when all this is over," Windy said, "he could dig them up."

"Maybe he couldn't display them again but at least he'd still have them."

"You suppose the police looked for them in his woods?"

"I doubt it. Dr. Wells isn't a suspect, I am."

"What do you think? Should we look?"

I drummed my fingers on the tabletop. "Right after the funeral."

"We should have plenty of time. Dr. Wells won't be home. He'll go to the burial at the cemetery, then to the luncheon for Lisa at the church. All that should take a couple of hours or more."

"Sounds like a plan," I said.

Twenty-one

By the time Windy and I found a place to park four blocks away from the church, a soft rain had started to fall.

We hopped out of the pickup, and I shivered.

Windy had brought an umbrella from home this morning. She opened it, and I ducked under it with her. She had tried to convince me I should go to the funeral incognito. Like wear mirror sunglasses and a stocking cap to cover my red hair. She thought Dr. Wells and Eric would not be happy to see me. That my presence might cause trouble, but I told her no way would I go to the funeral undercover. I was finished sneaking around. Sneaking around would make me look like a coward. Like I was afraid. Like I had something to hide. Like I was guilty.

Besides, sunglasses and a stocking cap would make me look conspicuous. Windy finally agreed that her idea was silly.

With its tall twin steeples, crosses at the top, and huge stained-glass windows, the United Presbyterian Church in the heart of downtown State Center reminded me of medieval cathedrals I'd seen in pictures.

Its bells tolled mournfully. The chilly rain, coming harder now, pelted hundreds of people as they crowded ahead of us through the church doors. Nearly all the older adults wore black, but the school kids wore mostly regular school clothes—jeans, slacks, shirts, and sneakers.

As we neared the church door, Windy said, "I'll bet nearly half the university faculty is here."

"And probably three hundred kids from school."

Right in front of the door someone gripped my elbow and pulled me aside, off the walkway onto the grass.

I turned sharply.

"Got some news for you, Billy-boy." Moody was smiling his evil smile. He was dressed in an immaculate uniform, his brown shoes bright despite the rain. He wore a clear-plastic raincoat, and a plastic cover like a shower cap protected his Smokey Bear cop hat.

"Figured out what happened to Lisa?" I asked. "Talk to her dad? Ask about suicide?"

Windy stood in the background but still within ear-shot.

Moody's smile broadened. "We found Rodney Wells's car on Highway two-eighteen, about sixty miles south of here. White GTO."

"Where is he?"

"Looks like his car broke down. Plenty of gas. He apparently hitchhiked."

"Find the guns in his car?"

"Didn't expect to. Why don't you tell me where you hid them? Make things easier for all of us."

"Can't help you."

"This Lisa Wells was a very popular girl," Moody said. "Look at all the people coming to her funeral. Once the media knows you slept with her before she died, everybody in this county is going to question you, Billy-boy. Just like me. Got a lawyer yet?"

"I won't need one."

"Be seeing you." He joined the stream of people pouring into the church.

"He's certifiable," Windy said.

———————

Windy and I stood in the packed church along the sidewall in a line of mourners that stretched from the front to the back of the church. I looked up and over my shoulder. I was standing underneath a stained glass window of Christ crucified on the cross. On the other side of the church, standing under stained-glass windows, stood another line of people, stretching from front to back. Other mourners filled the center pews, the balcony pews on either side of the church overlooking the altar, as well as the pews in the balcony over the church's entrance.

The church organ's somber tones and a soprano's plaintive voice blended together in "Amazing Grace."

Pallbearers—six girls from the varsity volleyball team, all dressed in black dresses—rolled the casket up the carpeted aisle on a silver-bright wheeled cart. A blue and gold spread that looked like silk draped the casket, a spray of perhaps fifty white roses balanced on its center.

My eyes scanned the front of the church. Dr. Wells sat stiffly in the front pew, a woman dressed in black and wearing a huge black hat sat next to him. I guessed the woman to be Lisa's maternal grandmother—Dr. Wells's mother-in-law—Lisa's only other living relative, besides her dad, she once told me. Ms. Jameison and other high school faculty sat up front as did other members of the girls' sophomore and varsity volleyball teams.

Eric and his parents sat in front, too.

And next to Eric sat Sheriff Henry Moody, whispering to Eric, their heads bobbing. I knew what they were talking about.

My gaze dropped to the carpeted floor.

I let out a deep breath and lowered my lips to Windy's ear. "How come you're not up there with the other girls?"

"They asked me this morning, but I told them I'd already promised to go with you."

"You didn't have to."

"I wanted to."

When the minister approached the podium, cleared his throat and spoke, I tried to blank out his words. I didn't want to hear what he had to say. No one had known Lisa like I had. But some of the minister's words filtered through, anyway: "…a tragedy for all of us…our hearts and prayers go out to her loved ones…especially her father who cherished her dearly above all other earthly creatures." Stuff like that is what I didn't want to hear, how her father loved her. "In the mix of emotions," the minister droned on, "…shock, disbelief, horror…one bright ray…she will live in our hearts always. And again in the resurrection from the dead…"

Tears hung from my eyelashes, and I brushed them away.

Wobbling up to the podium, a few teachers and students shared memories of Lisa, all validating her beauty, brains, talent. Ms. Jameison spoke. She praised Lisa for her hard work and determination to succeed as an athlete and student. She didn't mention the other side of Lisa Wells—the unhappy, frightened, vulnerable girl who wanted to escape her father. The girl who was experimenting with pot. The girl who may have committed suicide.

At the end of the ceremony, the minister said all the mourners were invited to the gravesite and then reminded them of the luncheon in the church basement. Then the organist blasted the church with the opening chords of the final hymn, "On Eagles Wings," and the pallbearers began slowly wheeling the casket back toward the entrance of the church.

I looked at Windy. She watched glassy-eyed as the pallbearers guided the casket down the aisle.

Starting at the front, nearest the altar, the mourners filed out of their pews to follow behind the casket, nearly everyone with a handkerchief in hand, dabbing at eyes, blowing noses, some crying out loud. But could anyone else feel worse than I did?

People standing with Windy and me along the side aisle waited patiently for the center pews to empty.

Suddenly Eric Benson stared at me from the center aisle, hate and fury burning in his eyes as he shuffled out of church with the other mourners.

"Eric's watching us," Windy said. "Maybe we should go out the side door, up by the altar. Avoid him."

"It's time I decked him."

"We don't want a scene at church—he looks like he's ready to start something."

"Won't be my fault."

"God, Billy, sometimes your stupidity blows me away." She grabbed my hand, pulled me across a row of empty pews to the center aisle, and dragged me toward the altar. "We're going out the side door," she said. "I don't want to be in the middle of a fight in front of church."

But as she said that, I watched her mouth drop open, her eyes fixed on someone or something behind me.

I turned.

Threading his way back against the crowd of people leaving church burst Eric—a bull—his face red, his fists knotted.

"I knew you'd try to duck out." Eric jammed his glasses up his nose. "I know what you did to Lisa!"

"What? What did I do?"

"Cut it out!" Windy said. "We're in church."

The last of the people leaving church turned their heads to watch.

"You killed her!" Eric whispered fiercely at me, a notch below the sounds of the organ music and the singing. "You slept with her, then killed her!"

"Shhhh!" Windy hissed.

The people stopped and stared. I don't know if they could hear us over the music and singing or not.

"I didn't kill her," I said.

"I just figured it out," Eric said. "It's the only possible answer. It's why you accused *me* this morning of killing her—"

"Eric, please…" Windy said.

"You were pointing a finger at me to get yourself off the hook. It's probably what you're telling the cops—*I* killed her."

"Eric," Windy said, "calm down."

"Truthfully," I said, "we think maybe Lisa committed suicide."

Eric shook his head so fiercely I thought his glasses might fly off. "You're trying to cover your ass," he said, "in every possible way. First *I* killed her. Now she committed suicide."

"She was giving things away—did she ever mention suicide?"

"We think it's a real possibility," Windy said.

"You're dead," Eric said to me. "So help me, the next time I see you alone, you're dead! Fucking dead!" His head bobbed up and down. "Fucking dead!"

"You tell me that one more time, you better do something about it."

Windy clutched my arm. "C'mon, Billy, we're out of here." She pulled me to the side door. "Out this way."

And with that Eric backed off.

A few people lingered at the doorway we were trying to escape through, staring, probably wondering what the exchange between Eric and me had been about.

"Excuse us, please," Windy said, and people stepped aside.

I glanced over my shoulder. Eric had disappeared from the center aisle, apparently rejoining the crowd leaving the church slowly behind the casket.

Outside, the sky hung low and gray, and rain continued to fall softly. People stood around on the sidewalk and on the grass, holding umbrellas, talking, wiping eyes, and blowing noses.

"Eric's gone crazy," Windy said.

I was trembling. I felt on fire. Even the rain couldn't chill me.

Windy popped up her umbrella. "Hey, you're shaking. Relax. Your face is practically scarlet."

I looked toward the street. Cars lined the curb in single file for the journey to the cemetery, the black hearse first, close behind it was a black stretch limo.

"Wait for me at my truck," I said.

"Where are you going?"

I spun away from her and ran for the street, dodging the clusters of people on the lawn and sidewalk.

"Billy!" I heard Windy cry. "Wait!"

At the street, I cut between the hearse and limo, halted, and peered through the limo's windshield into the back seat, looking for Dr. Wells. The limo driver frantically waved me away. The woman with the black hat and veil sat behind the driver next to Dr. Wells. The good doctor stared at me with wide eyes.

I marched to the limo's street-side back door, pulled the handle, and whipped the door open.

I don't know if people on the sidewalk were watching or not. Or if they could hear me. "Lisa committed suicide!" I yelled into the limo at Dr. Wells. "I have her journals and notebooks! I can prove it!"

"You're crazy!" he shouted back.

"You made the suicide look like a murder. I have every-thing—a suicide note!"

A muscle in Dr. Wells's cheek twitched. But he didn't seem to panic. The woman passenger next to him gasped and her black veil fluttered.

"I know the truth!" I said.

Dr. Wells waved me off with a swipe of his hand. "You're out of your mind!"

The limo driver yelled, "Get the hell out of here. Close that door!"

"YOU STOLE YOUR OWN GUNS!" I screamed, and backed away from the limo.

This time, Dr. Wells's face froze in wordless horror.

Reaching for the limo door, I slammed it shut, hoping the glass would shatter, and began to run past hundreds of gawking spectators. Maybe I was crazy.

Twenty-two

I ran the first three blocks back to my pickup, then slowed in front of the library, stopped, and turned around.

Windy was following, half-running, the umbrella still up. I waited for her, puffing as if I'd run a mile.

She caught up and said, "You've really lost it! I heard what you yelled at Dr. Wells just before you slammed the limo door. What else did you say to him?"

She held her umbrella over me.

"I told him I found Lisa's suicide note. I know he'd made her suicide look like a murder. I told him he stole his own guns."

Windy stared at me in disbelief. "We don't even know for sure if she committed suicide. Or that he took his guns and buried them."

"I don't think Rodney killed her. The cops would've found the guns in his car."

"Maybe he hid them along the roadside when his car broke down."

"Could be, but I doubt it."

"I wish you'd *think* before you do stupid stuff like this."

"Eric didn't kill her. Did you see his eyes blazing at me? He truly thinks *I* did it."

"We still don't know for sure if her death was a suicide."

"But I want Dr. Wells to go crazy with worry. You should've seen his face when I told him I knew that he stole his own guns. I think we can make him crack—I think I made him damn nervous."

"Oh, look," Windy said.

Three blocks away, the hearse pulled away from the church, the limo following, and behind it trailed an endless line of cars. Their headlights gleamed, and a little blue mortuary flag waved goodbye from the fender of each car.

The stream of cars didn't pass Windy and me standing on the street in the rain. A block before us, the line turned to its left and drove slowly out of sight, tall buildings blocking the view.

The light rain pattered off Windy's umbrella.

I felt hollow inside. My throat ached. Why hadn't Lisa asked me for help? I would have done anything.

Tears flooding my eyes once more, I turned and stumbled toward my truck.

Windy held the umbrella over me again.

"What are we going to do?" she said.

"Go home, change into lighter clothes. Check the woods. We'll probably have to swim across the lake."

"What if we don't find anything?"

"I'll break into the house if I have to."

"You really want to go to jail, don't you, Billy?"

"The message we found in that bag of pot means something: 'Under the desk an attic door.'"

At home, after I'd dropped Windy off, I hoped to slip in and out of the house quickly before Mom and Dad could ask any questions. When I parked my truck in the drive, I saw that Dad's car was gone. Hopefully, Mom and he were out.

I gathered Lisa's notebooks and folders from under my seat in my arms and hurried to the house. Mallard ran to meet me, wagging his tail, and seemed to sense my nervous excitement. The dog followed me to the door, barking.

Stepping inside the house, I cussed under my breath.

Mom was in the kitchen, starting supper. The kitchen smelled of tomato sauce and Italian sausage. Spaghetti for supper. She liked to let it simmer a long while. Another of my favorites.

"How was school today?" Mom asked as I started to duck down the basement stairs to change.

I halted. I couldn't ignore her. "Not good."

"You go to the funeral? I heard about it on the news."

"I went, lots of people there."

I headed down the stairs before she got another question off.

In my room, I shoved Lisa's things under the bed. Then I threw off my school clothes and jumped into cutoff jeans, T-shirt, and sneakers, no socks. Nothing extra. I had to swim Lake Wells in a hurry.

I closed my bedroom door softly behind me, looked up the stairs, and prayed Mom had poked her head into the refrigerator, digging for something, so I could get out the door before she knew I'd gone.

More bad luck.

She was waiting for me, framed in the doorway, a slotted spoon in her hand, pointed at me. "Where are you going so fast?"

I stood at the top of the stairway, shuffling my feet, all antsy. I needed to be on the road. "I've got something very important to do, Mom."

"Someone called for you earlier."

"Who?"

"He wouldn't say. He gave me his cell phone number. He said he wanted you to call him. And he said not to make any foolish mistakes. He sounded scary, Billy."

My breath caught. "A man with a deep rolling voice?"

"Yes. You know him? You want his number? What does he want?"

"I don't need to talk to him."

Mom shook the spoon at me. "Are you getting into more trouble again, Billy?"

"Mom, please…"

"Who is he?"

"I have to go. I'll probably miss supper. I—don't worry about me."

I dashed out the door and ran to the barn, where I grabbed a spade and shovel. I threw them into the back of the pickup. Mallard jumped into the cab as soon as I opened the door. I glimpsed Mom standing in the door-way. Shaking her head and looking fearful, she watched me speed away.

"Dr. Wells called me," I told Mallard. "I've really got him freaked. He wants me to call back. No way. If the guns are buried in the woods, he's probably totally freaked."

I zipped along the gravel road headed for Windy's house.

No need to tell Windy about the call. I didn't want her to freak, too.

———————

A half hour later, I parked the pickup off the road in the woods, and then Mallard, Windy, and I trotted down the gravel lane to Lake Wells. Under still, gray skies, the rain had turned into a persistent drizzle. Dr. Wells's house sat brooding on the hill across the lake.

I carried the shovel and spade. Windy hauled an inflated inner tube and a ten-foot piece of nylon cord.

Windy stored four inner tubes in her garage at home. We used them for tubing the Cedar River in the fall when the water was down. This one had a canvas seat laced to it where we set our cooler full of pop and sandwiches. I figured we'd use the tube to tow the spade and shovel across the lake. The trouble was the tubes in her garage had been deflated. I'd forgotten about that. I'd had to waste ten minutes going out of our way to the Parkview Kwik Stop to blow this one up.

When I reached the water's edge, I handed Windy the shovel and spade. I stepped into the chilly water up to my knees, shivered, and waded around in the thick, tall weeds, shoving them back with my hands. I was looking for the canoe I'd left here the other night after I'd fled Lisa's bedroom.

"No canoe," I said. "Didn't think there would be. Put the shovel and the spade on the tube. I'll tow it."

"How are we going to work the woods when we get there?"

"We'll start at the edge closest to the house. It was dark when Dr. Wells buried the guns. He would've had a flashlight, but I don't think he would've gone very far into the woods."

I figured it this way: the woods surrounded the house on three sides like a horseshoe, so we'd start at the tip of the horseshoe, near the water's edge, and cover ground about twenty yards deep into the woods. We'd work around the horseshoe until we reached the other tip and then make another twenty-yard sweep back, a little deeper into the woods. We'd look for freshly turned dirt, a patch of ground where the leaves have been disturbed. Any place where it looked like someone had been digging.

Windy tied the line to the tube, laid the shovel and spade on the tube, and shoved it into the water. "Are you serious about breaking into the house?"

"If we can't find any guns, I don't have a choice. C'mon. Let's swim across the lake."

Twenty yards out, Mallard was already swimming in circles. Dressed like me, Windy backed up the bank twenty steps, sprinted to the water's edge and dove in with a belly splash.

I waded out from the weeds and inched into water up to my chest. I held my arms high, shivered, and felt the goose bumps popping out on my arms and shoulders. For a reason I didn't understand, Windy was always able to swim in colder water than me. She swam thirty yards out, Mallard following, treaded water and shouted, "C'mon, chicken! The water's fine." She'd grabbed the line tied to the tube and had it in tow.

My teeth chattered.

I took a deep breath and plunged into the cold water.

Twenty-three

The woody terrain—mostly oak, maple, and hickory trees—was level with a few swales. Occasionally the trees thinned into almost a meadow. The tangle of vines, weeds, grass, and saplings that cover the ground in July had just begun its summer growth, which made walking easy. And with last fall's leaf cover still matted on the ground, I had no doubt that either Windy or I could recognize a spot where somebody had been digging.

But we'd been searching nearly an hour with no luck, and I now realized we might have taken on an impossible job. The trouble was the two of us simply couldn't cover every inch of ground. A hole to bury four or five guns need be only four feet long, two feet wide, and three feet deep. We might very well miss it.

Still, I clung to the theory that Dr. Wells, gun lover that he was, would not have dumped the guns in the lake. He would have buried them in the woods—if he had stolen his own guns.

Windy and I had worked our way deep enough into the woods now that we were out of sight of the house. When we'd started the search, I could see the place. No cars in the drive in back of the house. All quiet. I wondered if I should have broken into the house first, looking for an attic door under her desk and searched the woods later.

Windy worked the woods fifteen yards off to my left, stepping over downed tree limbs, pushing aside brush, eyes on the ground, head moving side to side, like watching a tennis match.

Mallard swept back and forth thirty yards ahead of me, belly sucked in, nose to the ground, and snorted as he inhaled the earth's scents. He probably thought we were hunting quail. I wondered if it had occurred to the dog that the fork and shovel Windy and I carried weren't guns. So far Mallard had flushed two rabbits but held his ground, quivering, and didn't chase them. At least he knew he was a bird dog when I was with him.

The drizzle continued to fall and a gray mist hanging in the woods wrapped itself around the dark trees. I kept shivering, wishing for warm, dry clothes, especially shoes and socks.

"Hey, look!" Windy squealed off to my left.

I swung my head her way. "What?"

"Look!"

I leapt a downed tree trunk and sprinted to the top of a rise, where she stood, pointing.

"You found something?" I was breathless.

"Morels," she said. "Look at them. They're everywhere on this little hill. We've had rain, then warm weather, now rain. Perfect. Look at them." Windy pointed her finger at the tiny sponge mushrooms poking their heads out of the ground. "There... And over there..."

"We're not looking for mushrooms, Windy."

"I know what we're looking for."

I scanned the area. "I think the depth we're into the woods right now, about fifty yards, is critical. I don't think Dr. Wells would've gone any deeper. Not at night. And he probably doesn't know the woods. He collects guns, he's a shooter, but I don't think he's a woodsman."

"Right."

"If we don't find anything on this pass," I said, "I'm breaking into the house to find that attic door under the desk."

"If you get caught, Billy, they'll hang your ass for sure."

"You don't have to go in. You can stay outside and warn me if someone's coming."

"What? One if by land, two if by sea?"

"Yell or something, I don't know. C'mon, we're wasting time. We'll come back another day to harvest Dr. Wells's mushrooms."

I looked for Mallard. He was behind us, working a swale Windy and I hadn't covered. Nose against the ground, head sweeping side-to-side, tail spinning, the dog capered around a ten-foot area in tighter and tighter circles.

Suddenly he halted, pounced, and started digging at the ground.

"What's he doing?" Windy said.

"He's on to something."

"Maybe it's a deer carcass."

"Probably a poacher dressed it and buried the entrails."

We ran down the hill to where Mallard was digging in the soft ground.

"Look at the overturned leaves and dirt around here," I said. "Someone was digging here before Mallard. And not too long ago."

"What is it, Mallard?" Windy said.

The dog barked, the hair along his back bristling.

I pushed him aside and scooped the loose earth away with my shovel. Windy sunk her fork into the ground.

"I hit something," she said.

My heart pounding, I scooped dirt with my shovel like I was a digging machine. Finally I glimpsed the colors blue and gold. I stopped.

"What's that?" Windy said.

"A towel? A shirt? I don't know."

I started digging again. I threw the dirt over my shoulder until I created a hole two feet deep, three feet long.

Mallard pranced back and forth, barking, back hair still standing straight.

"It's a plastic tablecloth from Saturday's party!" Windy said.

I stopped digging, my mouth falling open. "Oh my God!"

"Did someone wrap up all the garbage from the party and bury it out here? Is that what we've found?"

I pulled back. "I don't know. The smell's awful." I dropped my shovel. "Give me the fork." I poked a prong into the plastic, ripping a big hole in it.

A horrible, more terrible smell spewed from the hole. I dropped the fork and shrank back. Windy caught the smell, turned her face, and covered her nose. Mallard curled his lips, baring his fangs, and growled.

"It's a body," I gasped, and backed away from the hole.

I went totally cold, and nausea churned my stomach.

"Whose?" Windy said.

"I don't know." I was breathing so hard my chest hurt. "But it's a body."

I backed farther away and leaned against a tree. I tried to catch my breath but gagged. "I thought we might find the guns. Never in my wildest dreams did I think we'd find a body."

Windy pressed against me. Wrapping my arms around her, I felt her quivering.

"Whose body?" she said again.

"I don't know. You're shaking, too."

"You're sure it's a body?" she said.

"A leg, I saw a leg. And the smell. It's worse than a dead hog. I always heard humans smelled bad."

Mallard continued to prance around the hole, barking, pawing at the ground. I called him off, and the dog came running. I bent and scratched him behind the ears. "Good dog...good dog."

Mallard barked again.

"What are we going to do now?" Windy said.

"Move away from the hole—I can't think."

We clambered another twenty yards away until I lost sight of the spot through the trees. We sat hunched on the trunk of a fallen tree, Mallard sitting at my feet.

I shivered again in the cold drizzle. Windy's face was white, lips pale, spiky black hair flat. Raindrops dripped from her ears, nose, and chin.

I was suddenly shaking all over. I couldn't tell if it was from the cold and the rain or from what I'd just smelled and seen. A dead person buried in the woods behind Dr. Wells's house. A dead person wrapped in one of the blue and gold plastic tablecloths that had covered the picnic tables at Lisa's party.

Blue and gold, the school colors.

I tried to grasp the enormity of our discovery, and my mind reeled.

Was there a connection between Lisa's death and the death of the person half-buried thirty yards away from us?

Another person who'd been at the party?

Had I stumbled on to a real murder?

I hadn't heard of anyone who was at the party who was missing except—Rodney Wells!

Windy said, "It might be Rodney Wells."

I blinked. "I was thinking the same thing, but it can't be Rodney. The cops found his GTO sixty miles from here on Highway two-eighteen."

"That doesn't mean he drove it there. The cops found a gun in your pickup, but you didn't put it there."

My teeth started chattering. "W-we have to find out who it is," I said.

"That means—"

"D-digging it up and rolling it out of the plastic," I finished for her.

"I'm not sure I can."

"Me either," I said, and hugged myself with my arms and hands for warmth.

Suddenly Mallard pricked his hears and barked. Windy turned. "Listen!"

"What?" I turned with her. I hadn't realized it, but we sat only twenty yards from the edge of the woods.

"It's a car," Windy said.

As soon as the words escaped her mouth, I heard a car door slamming.

Someone had driven in and parked in the drive behind Dr. Wells's house.

I scrambled to the edge of the woods, Windy and Mallard behind me. I threw myself down behind a fat tree and Mallard lay next to me. I rapped the dog on the snout with my forefinger, a signal Mallard knew from duck hunting. Be silent. Don't bark.

Windy crouched behind her own fat tree, five feet away from me to my left.

Seventy-five yards in front of us, Dr. Wells's maroon Chrysler New Yorker sat in the drive in the drizzle.

I glanced at Windy. She bugged her eyes and shrugged. I knew she was asking herself the same question that was hurtling through my mind: *Why was Dr. Wells home so soon?*

Then I figured it out.

Dr. Wells had to go to the burial service at the gravesite. He couldn't skip that. He was already trapped in the limo with his mother-in-law. His skipping the burial would raise too many questions. But he must have skipped the luncheon and hightailed it back here as soon as possible. He probably said he was sick. Couldn't eat. Didn't want to visit with other mourners. Everyone would understand.

Next question: *What to do now?*

"Let's get the police." Windy whispered. "We've got a body for them."

"But we don't know whose body or what it means."

"Let them figure it out."

"I want the guns. The guns will prove Dr. Wells is guilty. You got your cell phone?"

She shook her head in quick jerks. "Us swimming in the lake, I thought it would be a nuisance. It's at home."

Suddenly the garage door rattled up, and I clamped my mouth shut. I rapped Mallard on the snout again, a reminder.

Dressed in hiking boots, jeans, sweatshirt, and a camouflage rain slicker, Dr. Wells emerged from the garage with a long-handled shovel in his right hand.

I held my breath.

Mallard's ears perked.

Windy pressed closer to the ground.

As my heart nearly pounded its way out of my chest, Dr. Wells marched straight across the yard and entered the woods, disappearing.

I waited silently until I was sure he wasn't doubling back through the woods toward us.

Satisfied, I inched on my belly across the wet ground closer to Windy.

"Did you see that?" I said. "He's got a shovel. He's going to dig up the guns."

"Let's get out of here and call the police."

"You go. I'm staying."

"If we get them now, the police will be here in time to catch him."

"Uh-uh. He might drive off with the guns before the

police get here and dump them someplace where they'll never be found."

"How are you going to stop him from driving off?"

"I'll think of something."

Windy sat up and shook her head fiercely. "Billy, don't you see, he's going to know someone else was there digging before him. If he sees you, he'll know you were the digger. He might kill you."

"I'll handle it."

"Damn you, Billy O'Reilly!"

"Phone the police from the Tastee-Freez. It shouldn't take you more than twenty-five minutes to get there. Tops. Tell them there's a body buried in the woods behind Dr. Wells's house."

"Like they'll believe me."

"Tell them it's Rodney Wells. That'll bring them running." I shifted to my knees and dug in my cutoff pockets for my keys. "Here…" Suddenly out of the corner of my right eye I glimpsed movement. "Duck!"

We both hunkered down behind Windy's tree. Mallard growled deep in his throat, and I thumped my forefinger off the dog's nose again. Dr. Wells marched back across the yard headed toward his car, his arms cradling a three- to four-foot long bundle wrapped in blue and gold plastic. On top of the bundle he balanced the shovel.

The guns! Oh, wow!

I clenched a fist and pounded it in the air.

I'd been right!

I fought the urge to run across the yard, tackle him, and pulverize him. But I realized the sensible thing to do was to wait for the police. Let them catch Dr. Wells in the middle of his mission—getting rid of incriminating evidence.

"He's got the guns," I whispered.

Windy nodded.

I watched breathlessly as Dr. Wells opened the back door of his New Yorker and lowered the bundle into the car.

"Get the police," I said. "Pick up the fork and shovel. Leave them on the bank down by the lake."

"Come with me, Billy…"

"You go," I said. "I'll be all right."

Twenty-four

Flat on the ground behind a tree, Mallard next to me, I watched as Dr. Wells popped the New Yorker's trunk open, reached in, and hauled out a three-foot roll of clear plastic.

Plucking something from his pocket—a penknife, maybe—he cut a hunk of plastic off the roll and laid the piece in the trunk. He raised the garage door, disappeared a moment into the garage, then reappeared pushing a wheelbarrow.

Lisa's white Grand Am sat in the garage.

Dr. Wells lowered the garage door, then laid the shovel and roll of plastic in the wheelbarrow.

I had no doubt Dr. Wells intended to dig up the body in the woods, wrap it in more plastic, haul it from the woods in the wheelbarrow, and dump it into the trunk of his car.

Where Dr. Wells intended to get rid of the evidence, I had no idea. Maybe the Atalissa quarry. That would be as good a spot as any. Plenty deep.

I tried to estimate how long it would take the police to get here. Fifteen minutes for Windy to run through the woods, swim the lake, and reach my pickup. Ten minutes to drive to the Tastee-Freez. Five minutes to make the call and to make the person she talked to understand a body lay buried in the woods behind Dr. Wells's house.

How quickly would the cops respond?

Would they respond?

Or would they think Windy was crazy?

If the cops responded instantly, it might take them fifteen or twenty minutes to get here. Total elapsed time: forty-five minutes. If everything went right.

Windy had left five minutes ago.

Dr. Wells could dig the body up, if he could stand the smell, have it loaded and be out of here in fifteen minutes. The cops would get here twenty-five minutes after he'd left.

Not good.

I smiled as a brilliant plan formed in my mind. I knew exactly how to trap Dr. Wells.

As the doctor raced with the wheelbarrow across the lawn toward the woods, Mallard and I inched deeper into the trees, circling away from the body, working our way back to the edge of the woods again.

How would Dr. Wells react when he saw someone had been digging there before him?

Would he race back to the house?

Probably not.

He'd have to stay there and complete the digging. He had to get rid of that body no matter what.

When I felt sure Dr. Wells was deep enough into the woods to be at the hole, I picked up a twig, then sprinted seventy-five yards through the drizzle across the yard to the driveway, Mallard galloping beside me.

I'd never run harder nor faster in my life.

I halted in the drive. I knelt at the Chrysler's driver's side back tire. Breathing hard, my hand shaking, I let the air out of the back tire with the twig.

Psssst!

Then the front tire.

Psssst!

Two tires because Dr. Wells could replace one flat tire with a spare.

When I finished, the car listed to its port side like a ship at sea full of water, about to capsize.

I glanced over the hood of the car. No Dr. Wells barging from the woods.

I inched open the car's back door, stuck my hand in, and ripped a hole in the blue and gold plastic.

The smooth wooden stock of a shotgun or rifle lay exposed.

Yes! I clenched a fist and almost screamed the word out loud.

I closed the car door softly.

Now the car in the garage. Lisa's Grand Am. I had to let the air out of two of its tires. Dr. Wells would be without wheels. No way could he haul guns and a body anywhere. Mallard and I could hide in the woods until the cops arrived, watching the frustrated doctor storm around his car, trying to figure out what to do next.

If he tried to hunt me down in the woods like a rabbit, I'd outsmart him. Outrun him.

I grabbed the garage door handle, twisted, and lifted, but the door didn't budge. I cursed. I twisted and jerked the handle again.

The damn door was locked.

Oh, man! Shit!

I hadn't counted on that.

I'd never be able to break in a front, back, or side door of the house. Dead bolt locks secured them all.

No time for a debate in my mind.

From among the flowers along the side of the house, I picked up a rock the size of a softball. I raced up the steps to the deck outside Lisa's bedroom, Mallard behind me.

I whipped off my T-shirt and wrapped it around the rock. I hoped my T-shirt would help dull the sound of the rock's crashing through the glass door. Though I suspected

Dr. Wells was too deep in the woods to hear glass breaking at his house, I needed to take every precaution.

Stepping back, holding the rock in my right hand alongside my ear like a shot-putter, I launched it through the glass door. The glass shattered into a million pieces—shiny pebbles, jagged daggers—and splattered everywhere on the white carpet.

I could get to Lisa's car by going through the house to the kitchen, then to the garage.

Nearly all the glass had broken out of the door except for jagged pieces on the sides and at the top and bottom. I unlatched the door from the inside, and slid it open. When I stepped into the bedroom, I could hardly breathe. A million memories of scents, sounds, and sights rushed in on me.

I unraveled my T-shirt from the rock, shook the glass pebbles off it, and slipped it over my head. My chest heaved.

Then my mind replayed Lisa's cryptic note: *Under the desk an attic door.*

My sneakers crunching on shards of glass, I crossed the room and stared at Lisa's desk. It was all white like the bed, dressers, and vanity table. A computer and printer sat on the desk. Bookends supported a dictionary, thesaurus, and several hardcover fiction books: *Moby Dick, Crime and Punishment, Gone with the Wind.* Everything sat in its assigned spot.

Pulling back the chair, I pictured in my mind the outside of the house. A peaked porch roof adjoined Lisa's corner bedroom on the north side. Lisa's desk stood against the peak's inside wall. The deck circled the south, east, and west sides of the house.

Dropping to my hands and knees, I crawled into the desk's leg space, and my heart skipped when I spotted a two-foot wide, three-foot tall piece of unfinished plywood standing against wall.

I shoved the plywood aside—the back of the desk held it up—and peered into the dark crawl space in the attic above the porch.

A secret room?

Lisa must have cut the hole in the wall with a saw. Then covered it with this hunk of plywood.

I stuck my head and shoulders through the opening and caught the sweet fragrance of marijuana mixed with incense.

My skin crawled.

I needed a light.

I felt around on the floor. If this was Lisa's secret room, her sanctuary, she must have had a light somewhere. Sure enough, I found the end of a drop cord, maybe a lamp cord. I plugged it into the outlet behind Lisa's desk, and her secret room flooded with lamplight.

What I saw made my breath catch.

The room was ten feet long with a peaked five-foot-high ceiling, hundreds of roofing nails sticking through. Plywood lay across the rafters and on top of the plywood lay a mattress for a single bed and a pillow. My eyes picked out two empty Jim Beam bottles and two ashtrays with roach butts in them.

Lying on the pillow was a white binder. I crawled in across the plywood to the mattress and picked up the three-ring binder that held perhaps five hundred pages. My hands trembling so bad I could hardly open the book, I recognized Lisa's handwriting and knew instantly what I'd found: her diary.

I flipped pages, stopped at one near the end, and read hurriedly, my eyes darting, hoping I'd spot something about suicide. But I got stuck on the first page. I read:

> *"Billy, you're trembling," I said. "Are you scared, sweetie?"*
>
> *"A little...your dad...?"*
>
> *I smiled when he admitted that, his face all red. He's so big and handsome and bashful, so much like a little boy, my heart breaks when I think about sleeping with him.*
>
> *"I told you Daddy's out of town," I said. "The maid goes home at nighttime. We're safe." I kissed him. "You have such sweet lips, Billy..."*

I slammed the book closed and clutched it to my chest. My face flamed. I finally possessed what I'd wanted so desperately, something written in Lisa's hand that might confirm she committed suicide, but at the same time her diary apparently contained a detailed record of our secret meetings. For the cops or anyone else to read. What fun everyone would have.

I spun around on my hands and knees to crawl out of the room, but I lifted myself too high—a roofing nail stuck me in the head.

"*Ouch!*" I cried, and swore.

The sharp pain snapped me back to the reality of where I was, what I was doing, the danger I was in. I had to get out of here.

I had no idea how much time I'd spent in Lisa's secret alcove. Five, six minutes maybe. Dr. Wells might be returning from the woods with the body. Seeing the flat tires on his car, he'd know someone lurked around the house.

I had to get the hell out of the house and dive back into the woods, leaf through the entire diary, and if it said anything about suicide, give it to the cops when they got here.

Where's Mallard?

My heart gave an anxious beat. I crawled out from under the desk. I stood. My eyes scanned the room.

No Mallard.

I curled my tongue, pursed my lips, and whistled softly.

Had the dog flushed out Lisa's cat and chased it outside? Or through the house?

Lisa's bedroom door was open when I'd broken in. The cat often slept on Lisa's bed or hid in her closet. It might have run downstairs, Mallard in hot pursuit, but I was so preoccupied I hadn't even seen or heard the dog give chase.

Setting the book on Lisa's bed, I edged to the doorway and looked up and down the hallway. I whistled again. Softly.

Mallard could hear the softest whistle practically a mile away.

He wouldn't case a rabbit, but he'd chase a damn cat.

But what if Dr. Wells were outside with the body, saw the flat tires, and then heard my whistling in the house?

Time's running out, Billy.

I tiptoed down the hall to the stairs, where I could look down to the living room. One more whistle. Then I was out of here. Mallard would have to be outside.

But the whistle never escaped my lips. At the foot of the stairs, dripping wet and muddy, his face grim as stone, Dr. Wells raised and aimed a shiny revolver at my head.

Twenty-five

Fear froze me in my tracks.

"Walk down the stairs slowly." Dr. Wells's deep voice knifed through the deadly silence.

I raised my hands without being told, but I couldn't move my feet. They felt riveted to the floor.

"Now!" Dr. Wells's dark eyes glared at me. "Down the steps slowly. Where's the girl?"

"What girl?"

"Your stupid dog's outside chasing Lisa's cat."

I lurched down the steps, afraid of falling, wanting to

reach for the banister for support but afraid of lowering my hand.

"The girl?" Dr. Wells insisted.

"There's no girl." My voice sounded strange, a voice trembling with absolute fear, a voice I'd never heard from myself before. I reached the bottom of the stairs. My knees shook, and a chill slithered down my spine.

"Got no time for games." Dr. Wells moved back and waved me away from the steps. "I saw fresh footprints in the dirt. I tried to warn you—I thought you might be stupid enough to show up here."

"It's the best move I've made."

"The small prints belong to the girl. You sent her for the police, didn't you?"

"What girl?"

Dr. Wells's face was the face of a desperate man. His lips set in a grim line, ashen skin stretched across his cheekbones, dark eyes gleaming, he looked totally freaked. Just like I'd hoped.

But his face was the face of a man who had to kill me.

I licked my lips, and a knot of fear twisted in my stomach.

I wasn't going to die before I pumped him full of more fear. Made him crack. "I know all about you. I read Lisa's diary. I have it at home. Everyone's going to know."

"You have nothing at all! That's why you're here. *You have nothing!*"

"If anything happens to me, my parents will give her diary to the cops."

Dr. Wells sneered. "If you have anything, it's fiction. Lisa always bogged herself down in fantasy—one of her weaknesses."

"A body buried in the woods, your guns—they're not fiction. You'll never explain all that to the cops."

"You buried the guns. I caught you stealing again, I killed you."

"No one will believe you. Nothing adds up. Why would I bury the guns in your woods? Whose body did you dig up?"

"My word, a sympathetic sheriff's ear—it'll add up. You're already a murder suspect."

"You're insane."

Muscles in Dr. Wells's jaw quivered. He clicked the revolver's hammer back. "You destroyed Lisa."

I began to shake again. That knot of fear in my belly clenched, and I felt sweat slide down my back.

"Lisa was the radiant daughter," Dr. Wells said. "I was guiding her toward a brilliant future."

"You were smothering her."

"You're dead, William."

Suddenly Mallard's frantic bark came from upstairs.

As unexpected as an ambush, Lisa's cat streaked down the stairs, and Mallard scrambled down the hallway ten feet behind it.

Dr. Wells jerked the gun and sighted the dog—a reflex action, his sighting my dog, a moving target.

Eight feet separated Dr. Wells and me. I ducked low and dove hard for Dr. Wells's knees. The gun fired, sounding like a cannon's roar over my head.

I smelled gunpowder, expected to feel pain but felt nothing except the crush of my shoulder into Dr. Wells's knees.

He swore.

He crashed backwards into a grandfather clock, shattering glass, the clock *bong! bong! bonging!* as it toppled over onto us.

As we rolled across the floor, I scrambled to grab the gun in Dr. Wells's hand—it fired again, the roar ricocheting in my ears.

Sucking air, gritting my teeth, gathering every atom of strength I possessed, I tried to wrench the weapon out of Dr. Wells's grip, but I realized with horror he was a powerful man.

While both my hands clutched his gun hand, Dr. Wells slowly forced my arms to bend so he could point the gun's muzzle at my forehead.

I felt the muscles in my neck and arms bursting.

Where's Mallard?

Why wasn't the dog chewing Dr. Wells's head off?

As I writhed on the floor, losing the test of strength, I slammed my knee into Dr. Wells's groin—a crushing jolt, I hoped.

He gasped and his eyes nearly popped out of their sockets.

The gun fired once more.

The explosion's heat burned my eyes. The gunpowder's stench clogged my nose, and the roar nearly burst my ears. I jerked back and cracked my head on the sharp corner of something. A coffee table?

Suddenly my brain felt bruised, and I seemed to be slipping off the edge of the world into darkness.

Another gun blast jolted me.

Louder.

Closer.

Am I dead?

The pain in my head screamed, and somewhere in my scrambled brain I heard a voice.

"Dropthefuckinggun!"

Windy's voice. Shrill. Screaming.

"Billy, are you all right? Can you hear me?"

Windy's voice again. Shaky.

I lay on the carpeted floor, feeling as if I were floating on clouds. Was I waking from a sleep? The dead? I raised my head and opened my eyes. My head was bursting with pain. The room spun.

I blinked, trying to focus my eyes.

The smell of gunpowder hung in the air.

I propped myself up with my hands, my eyes fluttering open.

Windy's voice said, "Are you all right, Billy?"

Astonished to find her standing over me, a shotgun in her hand, I squeezed my eyes shut. I couldn't remember exactly what had happened. Or what was going on.

I said, "What are you doing?"

Windy waved the gun at someone doubled up in a fetal position on the floor. He was holding himself, his face warped like an ugly mask.

"Making sure the good doctor doesn't go any place. You must've cracked him a good one. He can't stand or talk."

A memory came oozing back, clear and frightening. "Where's Mallard?" I wobbled to my knees.

"I haven't seen him."

"Where'd you get that gun?"

"Dr. Wells's car. I heard shooting."

I sat back on my haunches, my head pounding. "I think Mallard's shot."

"Oh my God," Windy said. "Where is he?"

"At the top of the stairs."

I leaned on the coffee table. I stood. Then I climbed to the top of the stairs and found my dog lying motionless, bleeding on the carpet.

"He's hit!" I knelt and stroked Mallard's head. "There's blood all over."

I stood and whirled at the top of the stairs. "I'll kill you myself!" I screamed down at Dr. Wells.

"Get the dog into your pickup," Windy said. "I'll take him to the vet, and you can keep this gun on Wells till the cops get here."

"When the police arrive," Dr. Wells groaned, "you're both going to jail."

I said, "For killing you maybe."

"Billy, get Mallard into the pickup."

I stumbled down the hall, grabbed two thick white towels from the bathroom towel rack and wrapped them around Mallard. In a moment, the blood oozing from the dog's chest drenched the towels.

I rushed Mallard down the stairs and out of the house to my truck. The driver's side door was open. I laid him on the seat. Slammed the door closed.

I raced back inside the house. My hands trembled as I took the twenty-gauge Beretta from Windy. Dr. Wells sat sprawled on the floor, leaning against the couch, his head lying back on a cushion.

I raised the gun to my shoulder.

Windy cried, *"Billy!"*

I sighted down the barrel and flicked off the safety with my forefinger. I spotted the red bead at the end of the gun barrel between Dr. Wells's eyes.

He gaped in horror.

"Billy, don't!"

"Move or say a word," I said to Dr. Wells, "and you are dead. For sure!"

Twenty-six

"I need to get a few more things straight," Moody said, leafing through his notebook.

"I've told you everything a hundred times," I said. "I want to call the vet."

"Your girlfriend already called. Your dog's alive."

"Barely. And I want to call my folks."

"I'll take you home in a minute."

We stood outside in front of Dr. Wells's house. It was six-thirty. The drizzle had stopped, but gray clouds still hung in the sky, and a chilled breeze blowing off the lake raised goose bumps on my arms.

I'd washed Mallard's blood off me, but it still stained my shirt. If Mallard died, I'd make Dr. Wells eat the T-shirt. Before I killed him.

Four cop cruisers sat in Dr. Wells's yard. Inside the house, the cops had been digging in the walls and ceiling to find the bullets Dr. Wells had fired. Windy had fired the fourth and final shot I'd heard, a blast from a shot-gun, stunning Dr. Wells and me, blowing an expensive oil painting of a ship at sea off the wall.

I didn't know where she'd gotten the shells.

Smart girl, Windy. One of a kind.

The cops found Lisa's diary on her bed. I saw one of them pawing through it. Eyebrows raised.

Moody said, "Let me get this straight. You broke into Lisa's locker this morning, found a bag of marijuana with a note in it: 'Under the desk an attic door.'"

"That's right."

"And you threw the marijuana away."

"Right."

Moody's lips curved into a threatening smile. "I can nail you for withholding evidence and destroying evidence, ever think of that, Billy-boy. Both felonies. How do you like that? See what you've done, messing in police business."

My head dipped. My heart thumped. I didn't have any answer.

"The note's where?" Moody said.

"In the glove compartment of my truck, I think."

Moody frowned. "Lisa meant the note for school officials

or the police. If she intended it to be a suicide—I'll never be convinced of that—she wanted us to know about it. Whatever happened, she wanted to let us know why. Maybe she was trying to save your ass so we'd know you weren't involved in whatever she decided to do."

I closed my eyes a second. *Oh, wow.* I'd never thought of that.

"Breaking into her locker, her room—not smart, Billy."

"Would you have taken the message seriously?" I said. "Or blown it off? Would you have searched under Lisa's desk for an attic door?"

He didn't answer.

"Probably not," I said. "You were too convinced I'd killed her—and that's why you didn't get to her locker before Windy and me."

"Look, Dr. Wells is being booked, and Lisa's diary will be read from cover to cover, for what it's worth."

"It'll be worth plenty."

"And we now know Rodney Wells did hitchhike. This afternoon the guy who gave him a ride when his car broke down came in to tell us what he knew. A concerned citizen. When I have more information, you'll read about it in the papers."

"Thanks."

Moody'd already told me that the body in the wheelbarrow was Rodney's.

"What I'm telling you right now," he said, "is that

tampering with evidence, trespassing, breaking and entering—all are serious crimes, Billy-boy."

"Did I have a choice? You'd never have found those guns or Rodney's body." I sighed. "Take me home, okay?"

When Moody drove into the drive at my house, I said, "Want to talk to my dad? Tell him I didn't kill Lisa. I didn't steal the guns."

"Don't push your luck, boy. That your truck there? Let's have a look in the glove compartment."

"Help yourself."

"I want Lisa's notebooks and other things, too."

As soon as Moody and I stepped out of his cruiser, Mom and Dad came rushing from the house. Mom threw her arms around me.

"Windy was just here, from the vet's. She left your truck." Mom wiped tears from her eyes. "She told us what she could. She looked scared and tired. She wanted to go home. Dad took her. He just got back. Are you all right?"

"I'm fine," I said. "Got a headache, that's all. What did she say about Mallard?"

"The doctor won't know for a day or two."

I shuffled into the house, dragged Lisa's notebooks and folders from under my bed, and hauled them back out for Moody.

Dad had followed Moody over to my truck. "What are you looking for now? More evidence to frame my son?"

Moody pulled a slip of paper from the glove compartment, read it, and slipped it between the pages in his pocket notebook. "I'll tell you one thing, Will, if your son hadn't acted so irresponsibly, he wouldn't be in the deep trouble he's in now—tampering with evidence, breaking and entering—"

Dad cut him off and smiled. "That's no trouble, Henry. Yesterday he was a robbery and murder suspect."

———————

After I showered and changed clothes, I ate supper late while Mom and Dad sat at the table with me. I tried to fill in the gaps in Windy's story. She hadn't known about my letting the air out of the tires on Dr. Wells's car or my breaking into Lisa's room and finding her secret hideaway and her diary.

Mom and Dad sat with their mouths open as I talked. I hadn't realized how hungry I was. As I told the entire story, I shoveled down three plates full of spaghetti. "I had only a few seconds to leaf through Lisa's diary," I said, finishing off my final plate. "But I'm sure she must've written in there she was going to kill herself."

"How awful," Mom said.

"They need to lock her father up forever," Dad said.

"I appreciate your standing by me."

"We'd stand by you no matter what," Mom said.

"Lisa was like a brand-new color to me," I said. "For a while, at least. I guess that's why I got so involved."

Mom got up, reached on top of the fridge for an envelope, and set it on the table next to my plate. "This came in the mail for you this afternoon."

My eyes focused slowly on the oval handwriting.

"It's from Lisa," I mumbled, barely able to speak.

"Thought so," Mom said.

"Open it," Dad said. "What's she got to say?"

"Will, it's personal," Mom said.

I stared at the envelope. It was postmarked last Saturday morning, 11:30 A.M., the morning of her birthday party. She'd probably gone to State Center to pick up last-minute things for her party and had mailed it then.

I rose from the table, clutching the envelope in my hand. "Excuse me," I said.

I didn't know where to go, what to do.

Was it the suicide note I'd been looking for?

She mailed it to me?

I excused myself and hurried down the basement steps to my bedroom and closed the door. I sat on the edge of my bed in the dark except for the green glow of my digital radio alarm. I held the letter in my trembling hands. I heard myself breathing deeply. Maybe I should throw the letter away.

Hadn't Windy and I already solved the mystery of Lisa's death? I no longer needed proof she'd committed suicide, did I?

Yes, I did. I hadn't read about suicide in Lisa's diary.

I sniffed the envelope. Lisa's lavender scent invaded

my nostrils. I felt a crooked, sad smile creep across my face. My life had started unraveling with a note from Lisa.

I turned on the light on my night table. I took my penknife from my pocket and sliced the envelope open.

I unfolded the white stationary, drew a shaky breath, and read:

> *Dearest Billy,*
>
> *I'm so sorry for hurting you this way, sweetie. The few moments we had together were wonderful. Fabulous. Awesome. But by the time you get this, I'll be on a splendid journey that will take me to who knows where. I'm not even sure myself. I'm going to discover who I really am. I'm going to find a life of my own—all without Daddy. Don't grieve for me. I know what I'm doing. I didn't want you to love me. You understand why now, don't you? I didn't want to hurt you even more than I already have. I just want to say I'm sorry. Be pissed at me—I don't blame you. But don't feel guilty. None of this is your fault. I can't help what I have to do. Daddy's left me no other choice. Accept what's happened. Go on living. Be happy for me, Billy, I am. Sometime, maybe, we'll be together again.*
>
> *Lisa*

Imprinted across the note lay a bright red lipstick kiss from Lisa. Another kiss goodbye. The last kiss.

I couldn't believe what I'd just read.

Was this a suicide note? She didn't say anything about suicide.

I frowned. Read it again.

On a splendid journey...a life of my own...don't grieve for me—she must have been talking about suicide, but she must have been high when she wrote it. Totally spaced.

...we'll be together again.

Did she think we'd meet in heaven? I didn't know about her, but I had my doubts about getting there.

I stared at the lipstick kiss and fought the impulse to kiss it back. Instead, I replaced the note in the envelope and tucked it carefully under my mattress. I hoped Lisa's diary cleared up everything. Even if it detailed our times together.

I knew Mom and Dad were probably dying to hear what was in Lisa's note. But I wasn't sure myself what the note was saying, so I didn't go back upstairs to tell them, and they probably decided not to bother me, because no one came knocking at my door.

I lay flat on my back in bed, hands straight out by my sides, and dozed. Each time I awoke, I glanced at my digital clock. When the time read nine-thirty, I was sure Mom and Dad had gone to bed, so I stole up to the kitchen, sat at the table, and called Windy.

I asked about Mallard. Windy said he was still alive when she reached the vet's. Doctor Norman said he'd know a lot more by tomorrow morning.

I explained to Windy how I'd broken into Dr. Wells's

house and found Lisa's secret room and her diary. "I had time to only glance at it." I didn't tell her about Lisa's note. I had to get all this other stuff straight in my mind first, then maybe Windy could help me figure out what the note meant.

"Wells's got a lot of explaining to do," Windy said. "They'll get him for something."

"I think Lisa left that message in the bag of pot so someone would read it, find her diary, and then discover how bad off her life really was and what she intended to do about it, commit suicide."

"She probably wanted the police to find the message."

"She probably figured if her counselor or the principal found the pot and the note, they'd turned it over to the police. Not her dad."

"Right," Windy said. "And she couldn't leave her diary lying out around home—like on her dresser—for the police to find because chances are her dad would've found it first and destroyed it."

"She was smart. She had all her bases covered."

"Except she didn't know her dad would try to frame you."

"Who could've predicted that?" I leaned back in my chair. Scratched my head. "You saved my life. What brought you into the house with a shotgun?"

"I called the police and decided to drive back to Dr. Wells's house and park in the lane as close as possible so I could see—I didn't want to swim that stupid lake again.

When I parked, I saw Mallard streak by outside chasing a cat. I knew something was wrong. Mallard should've been hiding in the woods with you…"

"That was Lisa's cat—you know how he likes cats."

"I got back in your truck and when I drove up to the house, I heard gunfire."

"I thought I was dead, for sure."

"I knew there were guns in the back of Dr. Wells's car. I'd seen twenty-gauge shells in your glove compartment this morning. I loaded up and went into the house through the garage. The door was up."

"Did you see a body in a wheelbarrow?"

"Yes. Rodney Wells, I guessed. I jumped and nearly peed my pants."

"I don't think anybody knows exactly what happened to him."

"The good Doctor Wells probably does."

"Were the cops at your house?"

"For more than an hour. I had to tell them my side of the story over and over."

"What did your parents say?"

"Both thought we were pretty stupid taking matters into our own hands, though Dad said he was glad Wells got nailed. Mom agreed." I heard Windy yawn.

"Look," she said. "I'm tired. I have a physics test tomorrow first thing, I'm going to bed."

"I'm sorry I dragged you into this, but I've got something else to tell you…"

"I don't want to talk anymore, Billy."

"Just one more thing…"

"I'm beat."

Click!

I wanted to tell her about Lisa's note, but Windy hung up so abruptly I wasn't sure she'd even heard my apology. I shrugged and hung up the phone. She'd bailed me out when I'd needed her most, but she'd already told me emphatically several times she was going to stay pissed at me for the rest of her life. No doubt she meant it.

Twenty-seven

Mallard died during the night.

That's what the vet told me when I called early the next morning after I'd helped Dad with chores. I made arrangements with the vet to have his body cremated. I planned to take his ashes and toss them over our cornfields, where Mallard had flushed and retrieved probably over a hundred pheasants during the past four years. That's no lie.

Final exam days were Wednesday, Thursday, and Friday. Students were required to be at school only when they had a test scheduled. Graduation was set for Saturday in the high school gym at 1:00 PM.

I didn't eat breakfast the morning I got the news about Mallard, and Mom didn't try to force me. I lay on my bed in the dark, no Mallard on the floor beside me. I wondered if I was going to be punished for the rest of my life for the wrong things I'd done.

Mom and Dad had asked me this morning about Lisa's note. After I let them read it and told them how weird I thought it was, Mom said, "You should give it to the police, Billy. Maybe it means something you don't understand."

"You don't need an ounce more of trouble," Dad said. "Give it to the police."

"All right."

That same day, the story of Dr. Wells's arrest broke in the newspaper. I read it before I went to school. He was being held without bail in the county jail for the murder of his stepson. Moody said they were withholding more details until the investigation could be completed.

The story didn't mention my name or Dr. Wells's attempt to frame me. That was all right. I didn't ever want to see my name in the paper. I wondered what had happened to Dr. Wells to make him turn out like he did, so controlling.

At nine o'clock I dragged myself off to school for my chemistry test at 9:45. Shuffling through the front doors of school, I felt like a zombie, my brain a hunk of stone. I failed my chemistry test. I knew it when I handed the paper in.

After class, as I rummaged through my locker, trying

to straighten it out, Eric marched up to me. He looked pale but angry. "You ratted me out, didn't you?"

I faced him. "Ratted you out?"

"Don't play dumb. You know—"

"I threw the shit away, I told you. Neither Windy nor I said anything to the cops."

I imagined he was still hurting because of Lisa's death. Like me. In fact, we would always hurt. We had that in common. Would we always be enemies? I wondered again.

"I'm being watched," he said, and stabbed at his glasses with his forefinger, pushing them up his nose. "I think the cops have me under surveillance."

"How do you know?"

"It's a feeling I have—someone's watching me."

"All right. Look. I'm going to tell you something that might help you out."

"You're going to help me out?"

"If you'll let me."

"Why?"

I thought about that for a second. "Because I know Lisa wouldn't want you to get into trouble."

He eyed me suspiciously.

"The cops have Lisa's diary," I said. "She might've written something in there that might incriminate you."

"What diary?"

"Lisa's diary—"

"She kept a diary?"

"Listen to me! I don't think she'd say you're dealing,

or anything like that, but she probably wrote about getting high, and the cops might figure out you're somehow involved."

"*Fuck!*"

"So you need to be cool. You need to stop whatever it is you're doing—you need to get clean."

Eric wrung his hands. "You ever been bored?"

"When I'm bored, I take a walk in the woods, I canoe the Cedar River, I fish and hunt, I plow snow in the lane by my house."

"I mean *bored!* Like you can't stand your life. "

"How much of that shit are you doing?"

"I've got it under control."

"Doesn't sound like it. Sounds like you're paranoid."

"You swear you didn't tell anyone?"

"No one, I swear."

He wrung his hands again. "I'd like to believe you."

"Believe me. And I'm telling you, if you're going to save your ass, you've got to get clean—cold turkey. Lisa may have written something in her diary."

He stared at me though his thick glasses. I thought maybe he was going to say something like *Thanks for the warning.*

But he said, "Whatever!"

He whirled and stalked away. Man, his head was so screwed up I could almost feel sorry for him. In fact, I think I did. A lot.

———————

Thursday before I went to school for my Spanish test, I decided to take Lisa's note with me and drop it off at the sheriff's office in State Center, and I wanted to ask Moody if Lisa's diary revealed that she intended to commit suicide.

But Moody showed up at the farm to return Dad's .22 pistol. I met him at the drive, my backpack slung over one shoulder. The cop opened the door, eased out of his cruiser, and handed me Dad's gun in its case.

The morning was bright. Crisp. Doves cooed on the telephone and electrical wires leading to the house. Like always.

"Don't need that gun any longer," Moody said, and smiled thinly.

"Thanks. You read Lisa's diary yet?"

"Lots of interesting developments since I seen you last, Billy."

"Like what?"

Moody leaned against the cruiser's door. Crossed his arms. "Rodney's car broke down, just like we thought. He got out and hitchhiked. A guy picks him up, and Rodney promises the guy a hundred bucks if he'd take him home. For a hundred bucks the guy figures why not. He's going this way anyhow."

"Rodney probably planned to steal something that was worth a hundred or more to pay the guy off. A gun maybe."

"When they got home, Rodney tells the guy to wait. He has to go in the house to get the money. The guy waits and waits. He gets out of the car and goes up to the door, but when he does he hears a gunshot."

"Dr. Wells shooting Rodney?"

Moody held up a hand, a signal to be patient. "The guy's not looking for trouble, so he gets the hell out of there."

"How'd you find him?"

"He came in to us Tuesday after he sees Rodney's picture in the paper. Wanted to be of help. You don't find many citizens like that anymore."

"Dr. Wells really did kill Rodney?"

"The kid walked in on Wells when he's in the living room hunched over Lisa's body on the floor."

I felt my gut clutch. I stared at the ground.

"Rodney figures Dr. Wells killed her—the doc's got a smoking gun in his hand—and the kid also figures it's a perfect opportunity for blackmail. Get some big-time bucks out of the old man."

"Why is Dr. Wells holding a gun?"

"Wells and the kid struggle over the weapon, and Wells accidentally kills the kid—according to the doc. I don't think Wells minded too much—the kid was a pain in his ass, anyway."

"The gun should've been in Lisa's hand."

Moody traced an index finger across his mustache. "You're not as smart as you think your are, Billy-boy."

"W-what happened?"

"Lisa was no suicide."

I blinked. Swallowed.

"Her diary says she intended to run away," Moody said.

"Run away?"

"She had a wonderful life planned for herself. Away from her daddy. Great adventures."

I shifted my backpack on my shoulder and thought of Lisa's letter...*a splendid journey that will take me to who knows where.*

"All kinds of details in her diary," Moody said. "So here's a question for you, Billy: if she's going to run away, has a new life planned, why would she commit suicide?"

I was so confused I could hardly talk. "She wouldn't."

"Exactly. So we know there's no robbery, and we know Wells shot Rodney, so if a robber didn't kill Lisa and if she didn't commit suicide, the next question is what really happened to her?"

I felt stunned. Like an anvil had dropped from the sky and cracked me on the head. "I think I know. But I can't believe it." I could hardly force the words out of my mouth. "Dr. Wells killed Lisa?"

"Killed her accidentally, he says. Like he accidentally killed Rodney."

"I don't believe it. How the hell can he explain that?"

Moody looked up at the bright sky. Then at me with his dark eyes. "When you left Lisa's bedroom the other night and she goes down to the kitchen to turn off them motion lights, Wells hears her. They quarrel about you.

She tells him she's getting the hell out—she's running away. He stalks her through the living room and belts her. She crashes against a black-stone fireplace, hitting her head and dropping to the floor."

My stomach started to heave. I felt sick. "Dead?" The word was a croak.

"Wells thinks so. He can't revive her. No vital signs, he thinks. You know what the crazy bastard does next?"

I tried to swallow the sour bile rising in my throat. It was impossible for me to think. Totally impossible. I didn't *want* to think. I wanted to pull the plug on my brain.

"He shoots her," Moody said. "Shoots her through the heart."

"Jesus Christ!"

"Fakes the robbery. Leaves the weapon in your truck. Comes back, buries his stepson and his guns, and calls us about one in the morning."

Now I felt flat-out sick but managed to say, "Why'd he bury just one body? Why not bury Lisa, too? He could say both kids ran away. Something like that. Who would know? Problem solved."

"We asked him that. He didn't give a damn about Rodney, but he wanted a chance to mourn his daughter's death. He wanted her to have a grand funeral. Wanted her to be heaped with all the praise and honors she deserved."

I couldn't stand listening to this any longer. "He wanted everyone to think what a great father he was," I said.

My hand reached out for the fender on Moody's cruiser

so I could hold myself up. The gun case I'd been hanging onto all this time dropped from my hand to the ground.

"Busy night for Dr. Wells," Moody said.

I tossed my backpack on the ground and staggered to the front of the cruiser, where I bent over and threw up in the morning sunshine under a blue sky, my gut wrenching, my ribs bursting. The dry heaves mostly. I hadn't eaten any breakfast.

Finished, I kept spitting, trying to get rid of the sour taste, failing. Then I straightened and wiped my mouth with the back of my hand. My eyes felt brimful with tears.

"Serves you right, boy," Moody said. "You should've thought twice about getting involved with Lisa Wells like that."

"Too late."

Moody's lips glided into a pleased smile. "Bullets retrieved from both bodies were fired from the same gun. We've got Wells backed into a corner. We might offer him a plea bargain. Manslaughter in both cases instead of two capital-one murder charges."

"Will he agree to that?"

"He'd be a fool not to. No chance for a parole on a capital murder conviction—if he lives long enough for a parole." Moody shrugged. "He might try to cop a temporary insanity plea."

"If you saw him when he tried to kill me, insanity might be right on."

"Whatever happens," Moody said, "he'll most likely die in prison."

"How do you know he's telling the truth? That Lisa's death was an accident?"

"Our autopsy revealed massive head trauma that would be consistent with a beating or a fall that could've killed her. Like when her head cracked against the fireplace. But our medical examiner ruled she'd died from the gunshot wound."

"What...?"

"Right," Moody said. "She was probably alive—barely—but Wells didn't know it when he shot her through the heart."

"What an *ass*hole he is!" I wailed, and felt myself trembling with rage.

I wiped my mouth again with the back of my other hand, wiped the backs of my hands on my jeans. I picked up my backpack, unzipped a side pocket, and with shaking hands pulled out the envelope with Lisa's note in it. "Got something for you. Read it."

Moody took the envelope from me, plucked the note out, and read it, his eyebrows rising. Then he looked at the postmark. "You been keeping this from me, Billy-boy?"

"I was going to take it to you this morning, before school. That's why it was in my backpack."

Moody read the note again. Nodded thoughtfully. "Sounds like a runaway's note to me."

"Why are you telling me all this?" I could hardly breathe.

Moody hitched his thumbs in his belt. "So you know you're not the bright boy you think you are—some of this won't be in the paper—and so you know police work is best left to the police. And so you know I'm still in charge around here." He poked himself in the chest with a finger. "Me. Cedar County Sheriff Henry Moody, I'm in charge."

I was trying to stop trembling. Trying to breathe. I wanted to remind him without Windy and me he probably would never have found Lisa's diary. But I didn't.

"Some good news for you in all this, Billy."

"What?" I finally caught a deep breath. Blew it out slowly.

"We're not charging you. You know, like tampering with evidence, breaking and entering. All that stuff. We're keeping our focus on Wells."

"Thanks." I rubbed my forehead. Felt sweaty. "I appreciate it. So do my folks."

"DA's choice, not mine."

"Thanks again. Anyway."

"Where are your folks?"

"In town, grocery shopping."

"Your dog?"

"Dead."

"Too bad."

Like you care.

"Stay out of trouble, boy. And tell your daddy I still haven't forgot—I owe him."

"I don't think he's worried."

Moody smiled, that evil glint in his eyes flashing. "Interesting reading, the girl's diary. You're lucky reporters haven't got a hold of it. Lots of juicy details in them pages."

"What will happen to her diary?"

"Her old man can enjoy it in jail."

And with that Moody climbed into his squad car and drove away, down the gravel road and out of sight. I hoped I'd never see him again.

That afternoon, after school, after failing my Spanish test, I staggered home, collapsed on the couch in the living room, and told Mom and Dad the whole story. They each grabbed a hand, pulled me to my feet, and hugged me fiercely. "We love you, Billy," they said. I felt humbled.

———

At first, I figured everyone in school knew about Lisa and me. Rumors like that run through school like wildfire, but though I thought I felt kids staring at me, whispering behind my back, no one said anything to me. Kids greeted me in the halls like always, and I tried to smile and say regular things: "What's happening, man?"

No one came up to me and asked, "How was she, dude? How many times did you do her? Did she get naked?"

So I figured maybe kids didn't know. Or they didn't have the guts to ask. I wasn't sure which.

Before I took Ms. Jameison's American lit test Friday morning, my last one, she stopped me at her classroom door and talked to me in the hall, privately.

I told her about finding Lisa's diary, getting a letter from Lisa, and what Moody revealed about Lisa's death.

"It's all so tragic," she said. "So bizarre."

"Why did her dad keep such a stranglehold on her?"

"Lisa's mother died during childbirth. Did you know that?"

That surprised me. "No. She would never tell me anything about her mom. 'It's way too sad,' she'd always say. 'I don't want to talk about sad things when I'm with you.'"

"His first wife—Rodney's mother—dies in a boating accident, and he's left with an incorrigible stepson. Then his second wife dies in childbirth."

"He didn't catch a break, did he?"

"Not at all."

"I think I understand him a little bit."

"He probably felt he was losing control of everything important to him in his life. Except Lisa. Lisa he could control, and he thought he had a magnificent vision for her."

"But she didn't buy into it."

"She wanted to rebel," Ms. Jameison said, "but at the same time she wanted to please him."

"She tried really hard to please him, I think."

"She finally felt hopelessly trapped. She couldn't stand the conflict any longer. She felt running away was her best choice."

"She was into pot," I said.

"You're kidding? How do you know?"

"I found some in her locker. Eric Benson got her started."

Tears crept into Ms. Jameison's eyes. "I feel so guilty. I should've done something before any of this happened. I should've known."

I felt my own tears pooling in my eyes. "If only Dr. Wells had cut her some slack... He must've really freaked when he realized she was going to split."

"I can't feel sorry for him, not after what he did."

"Me either."

"Maybe someday I'll be able to forgive him, I don't know."

I shrugged. I hadn't even thought about forgiveness. Maybe a hundred years from now.

Ms. Jameison dabbed at her eyes. "You look so torn, Billy, but none of this was your fault."

"Because of me she went down to the kitchen to turn off the motion lights—I'll never forget that."

Ms. Jameison squeezed my shoulder. "Don't blame yourself."

"If I hadn't been in her bedroom that night, if she hadn't turned off the switch for me, she'd be on the road to somewhere. Free."

"She's free now—Dr. Wells would've found her. He has tremendous resources...and then her life might've been a greater hell."

"Maybe."

I sidled by Ms. Jameison into her classroom, where I failed my American lit test. I'm sure my GPA had dipped below a B, probably closer to a C.

At least I'd graduate.

I wasn't in jail. Wasn't accused of murder and robbery.

I knew the truth about Lisa and what had happened to her.

But I'd lost my dog.

I'd lost Lisa, too.

And Windy, my best friend, I'd lost her.

Twenty-eight

I'd looked for Windy during test days and had seen her at a distance down the hallway on Wednesday in a throng of kids as classes were letting out. I waved and tried to weave my way toward her through the crowd, but she disappeared. I hoped maybe she'd call me at home after school to find out about Mallard.

But she didn't.

I didn't call her, either.

When I hadn't heard from her by Thursday night, I suspected the worst. She really was going to stay pissed at me for the rest of her life.

I went looking for her Friday afternoon after I'd taken my American lit test. Just to make sure she knew I was sorry for the way I'd mistreated her. And to tell her what I knew about Lisa's death. And maybe to see if we could be friends again.

Don't make a fool of yourself, Billy.

She was shooting hoops alone on the basketball court at the Long Grove Park. It's a tiny park by a little creek with a shelter for five or six picnic tables; swings, a slide, and monkey bars for little kids; and a concrete basketball court for anyone interested.

I parked my truck in the street, jumped out, and reached back for Woody, an eight-week-old golden Labrador retriever.

A squirming ball of fur with a pink belly, Woody chewed my hand as I snapped a leash onto his collar. His chocolate-brown eyes looked bright and mischievous.

I set the dog on the ground and pulled him gently through the grass with the leash, but Woody balked and tried to sit, twisting his head side to side, biting the leash. I gave the leash several light snaps and Woody got the message. He trailed along, lifting his oversized paws high in the grass.

The afternoon was bright with sunshine but cool.

Dandelions had started to pop their yellow heads up everywhere in the grass. Lilacs bloomed by the shelter, filling the air with their scent.

Picking up Woody and holding him in my arms, I

sat on top of a picnic table someone had pulled out from under the shelter, my feet on the seat. I watched Windy working on her jump shot from fifteen feet out.

She wore white denim shorts and a light-blue sweat-shirt, the sleeves cut off.

She was a good athlete—quick, sinewy, though not very tall. She'd posted a record 275 digs for the volley-ball team last year, and I thought she was the team's most consistent server, time after time blasting line drives—like knuckle balls—over the net by a fraction of an inch. She was hoping to be the starting point guard on the varsity basketball team next year.

She canned seven shots in a row before she missed one, retrieved the ball, and saw me sitting there, watching. Without saying a word—"Hello!" or "Go to hell!"—she turned to the basket to resume shooting.

Then she did a double take.

She'd spotted Woody in my arms and strolled toward me, smiling, the basketball in her right arm.

"Let me hold him!" Dropping the basketball on the ground, she sat at the picnic table and held her arms out.

"Mallard's dead," I said, shifting the wiggly pup to Windy's arms. I explained about having him cremated. "I'm going to toss his ashes over the cornfield behind the house."

Windy nodded solemnly. "I'm sorry, I really am. I loved that dog. Just like he was mine…"

"The vet gave me a telephone number of a guy in

Walcott who had labs for sale. That's where I got him. His name's Woody."

The pup was climbing up Windy's chest and licking the sweat off her cheeks and ears. "Woody, you need your nails clipped!"

"How you been?" I said, and tried to scrape up a smile.

Windy took her time answering. "Fine."

"You didn't call."

"Neither did you." Coolly.

I decided not to get into an argument about who should have called. "How'd you do on your tests?"

"Okay."

"I might've flunked all of mine...I mean, I know I did."

"That's a shame." She looked at me, genuine concern registering in her brown eyes. "I figured you'd have a tough time."

"I couldn't concentrate."

"One good thing about it is your name's not in the paper."

"I can't figure out why not."

"Because Dr. Wells's lawyers want to keep it quiet that he tried to frame you. Makes things look even worse for him. The cops told my dad that."

Then when I tried to tell Windy what Moody had told me about Lisa's death, she said she already knew the details. The cops' gossiping with her dad was her source of information. And I told her about the note Lisa sent me.

"First I thought it was a note from a suicide victim. Actually, it was a note from a runaway."

She scratched Woody's throat. He raised his head and licked her chin. "Um…I know something maybe you don't."

"What?"

"Eric was busted last night at his house."

"Busted? That figures."

"But only for possession. The cops actually thought he was dealing."

"Really?"

"But they found maybe an ounce of marijuana in his bedroom hidden in the toe of an old sock in the bottom of a laundry bag—they used a dog. They expected to find a bigger cache than that. Like a couple of kilos—four or five pounds."

"Unbelievable that he could be dealing, too."

Then I clued Windy in about my conversation with Eric on Wednesday. "I told him to throw the shit away. To quit cold turkey. I warned him."

"Well, if he was dealing, he must've flushed most of it, but he still tried to hoard some for himself."

"Maybe this will scare him straight."

"Ought to be a wake-up call to his parents—their boy Eric's got a problem. Maybe with help they can fix him."

I hoped someday Eric would remember I'd tried to warn him. We'd have no feud at all.

I propped my elbows on my knees. Laced my fingers. I had to ask this: "Any talk at school…I mean, about my sleeping with Lisa? My sneaking into her bedroom at night? Like how many times I did that?"

"None. It's not been in the paper. Eric won't say anything. Your hooking up with his girlfriend makes him look like a dork. Besides, he's got other things to worry about. I won't say anything."

"Thanks."

Windy scratched the pup behind the ears.

"I shouldn't have been so hard on her," she said. "The girl who had everything had nothing but a miserable life."

"I never dreamed how really bad off she was."

Woody went back to licking Windy's sweaty face. She cupped his snout with her hand. "Did you get a chance to read her diary?"

Windy released the dog's snout. He sneezed, then yawned, revealing his white, needle-like baby teeth.

"I read maybe a half page," I said. "I didn't see a word about suicide. Or running away." I shifted my weight on the picnic table. Stared at my laced fingers. "What do your parents think? I mean about me?"

"My dad says you made a terrible error in judgment."

"He's right about that."

"Everyone does that once in awhile, though. Mom says the girl must've tricked you. Somehow Mom thinks you're innocent in all this. She's always liked you."

"What do you think? I'll always be a dickhead?"

Windy looked up at the blue sky. "I don't know what I think anymore. I hated seeing you drool over her."

"I'm sorry. I never realized I was hurting you so much."

"Would it have made a difference?"

"I don't know. Lisa blinded me."

"You *let* yourself be blinded, Billy."

"All right, I admit that." I took a breath. "Will you go out with me tomorrow after graduation? We'll hit some parties."

Windy stared at me like I was crazy. Her mouth formed an O. Then she said, "What?"

"I'm asking you for a date. A real date. Not pretend like when we went to Lisa's party."

Windy set the dog on the ground and stood. She handed me the end of the leash. "Now I'm good enough for you? No thanks—I already have a date."

I felt my eyebrows collide. "Who?"

"Don't look at me like it's impossible. Kalen DeWitt, that's who."

"You're kidding! That drummer in the school band. Earrings. Pierced tongue. Different colored hair every other day. Green. Orange."

"I'll bet he's not a liar," she said. "I'll bet he's not humping someone every chance he gets. And lying about it."

I felt my face go up in flames.

"I like Kalen's hair," she said. "I like his earrings. I can't imagine what it must be like to kiss someone with a stud in his tongue."

I held up my hands in surrender.

I slid off the picnic table and stood.

She was right. I was a liar. Worse than a liar. Why would she want to go out with me? But I was still a good person, I thought, though I'd probably never be able to prove it to her.

I exhaled a big puff of air. "If I could put my life on replay, I wouldn't sleep with Lisa, but I did and I can't change that." Tears stung my eyes.

Windy stared at me wordlessly.

"What Lisa and I had," I said, "wasn't love. It was…it was wrong." I tried to breathe. "I'd…at least like to be your friend again…"

I halted.

God, I was going to cry right in front of her.

Why was I telling her all this?

All I'd been doing lately was crying.

Christ! I was going to be eighteen years old.

You fool, Billy!

I slid off the picnic table and stooped to pick up my pup. I hoped Windy couldn't see my face. I stood stiffly. I faced my truck and started in that direction.

I kept marching.

Her parents had named her Windy because she was born one night when we were all camping: her folks, mine, and me—a baby in diapers. A windy rainstorm had blown her folks' tent over on top of them, and her dad had had to rush her mom to a nearby hospital for their daughter's premature delivery.

I didn't need any more storms in my life. No more wind.

No more Windy!

I couldn't blame her for hating me, though. Her parents, either, if they did.

At my truck, I dumped Woody into the front seat and closed the door. I turned around. Windy had gone back to playing hoops, as if nothing had happened between us.

She didn't care about us.

Not anymore.

Did I still care?

If I drove away now, I was sure this would be the end between us. Positively. Did I really want that? Did I want to lose a lifelong friend? What would my life be without her? *Empty.* I hadn't thought of that before. I didn't want that.

I shambled back to the picnic table and stared at Windy. She stood under the net, basketball cradled in her right arm again. She stared back at me, unmoving. "What?" she said.

I think she was telling me the next move was mine. Not hers. She was right.

"You don't have a date with Kalen," I said. "Or anybody else, do you?"

Color crept into her cheeks. "I thought you were leaving." She started bouncing the basketball. Then held it.

"He's not your type, I know he's not. Why did you tell me that?"

"If you don't know why—I don't want to talk about it. Sometimes you are so—"

"*Stupid?* Is that what you're trying to say?"

"Just go—! Leave me alone, Billy."

I marched though the grass to the basketball court. I stopped in front of her—she didn't back up—but she dropped the ball and let it roll away.

"What?" she said again.

I suddenly grabbed her and wrapped her in a big hug, my chin planted on the top of her head. A moment passed before she hugged me back, but when she did, her arms clenched around my waist, and she pulled me closer, like this was a good place to be—in my arms. I wondered if she could feel my heart pounding against her chest.

When we released each other, I caught my breath and said, "Can we start over? Friends? Please? Is that a stupid idea? Please?" I was begging, but I didn't care.

"Where will that take us?"

"I don't know. But I'd like to see. Maybe to a new place. But we have to start as friends again."

Her voice, forced at first, softened. "I'm sorry I pissed you off just a minute ago, but I've been so mad at you. I mean, I really did think I'd stay pissed at you for the rest of my life."

"I know. I don't blame you. Does this mean we have a date?"

The faintest of smiles played around her lips. "All right."

I felt my face splitting into a huge grin.

Then Windy tilted her head and looked at me. After thinking a moment, she said, "Um...did you really think I wore too much makeup the other day?"

"When?"

"The other day when you picked me up."

"Oh, then."

I knew she was trying to avoid using Lisa's name and didn't want to mention her party. I felt the same way. I didn't want to be reminded of what had happened, either.

"You didn't wear too much makeup," I said. "You looked beautiful."

And then I kissed her on the forehead.

The End

About the Author

Jon Ripslinger is a writer and a former high school English teacher. He was a participant in the University of Iowa Writer's Workshop and is the author of dozens of published short stories and of three other novels for young adults. He lives in Davenport, Iowa.

Acknowledgments

A big "Thank you!" to the editing team at Llewellyn Worldwide, Ltd.: Andrew Karre, Brian Farrey, and Rhiannon Ross.

A big "Thank you!" also to Robert Brown and Sharene Martin of the Wylie-Merrick Literary Agency.

A special "Thank you!" to Rita Entsminger, who graciously reads my typo-riddle manuscripts.

Questions for Discussion from
Last Kiss

1. Early in the story, Billy feels that he is totally in love with Lisa. Is he really? Has he confused love and sex? By the story's end, what does Billy discover about the difference between the two?

2. Windy obviously doesn't like Lisa and the relationship Billy has with her. Explain why Windy stays by his side through this ordeal.

3. Billy learns a lot about his parents' relationship when they were teens. How does understanding his parents' relationship help Billy understand his relationships with Lisa and Windy?

4. Dr. Wells is an intelligent man, a president of a university, yet he makes fatal errors in parenting. Discuss these errors and how Dr. Wells might have handled the situation with his daughter in a better way, thereby avoiding this disaster.

5. What happened early in Dr. Wells's life that would turn him into a desperate man who would try to frame Billy for murder and shoot his own daughter through the heart to hide her accidental death?

6. What will eventually happen to Eric? Explain your answer.

7. Do you think Henry Moody will ever forgive Billy's parents? Do you think he should?

8. Do you think that Lisa truly loved Billy? Or was she using him like he suspected later?

9. Do you think parents putting pressure on their children, like Dr. Wells put on Lisa, to succeed is a good or bad thing?

10. Do you think Billy did the right thing by investigating the case himself? Or should he have gone to an authority figure and told them what he suspected?

11. By the story's end, Windy seems to have forgiven Billy for his insensitivity toward her feelings, and the two become friends again. Do you foresee a deeper relationship developing between the two young people? Explain why or why not.

12. If you were Windy, would you have forgiven Billy?

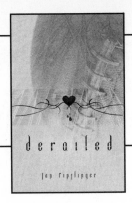

Derailed

JON RIPSLINGER

Everyone likes Wendell "Stony" Stoneking. He's the star of his high school football team and when he graduates, there's a job in the gravel quarry waiting for him. Then he meets Robyn, a single mom with a dark past. Suddenly Stony is bothered—not only by the violence Robyn has endured, but by the danger she could put him in. For the first time, Stony reflects on his life, his broken family, and the dizzying notion of a wide-open future.

ISBN: 978-0-7387-0888-1
5 ³⁄₁₆ x 8
288 pp. $8.95

Check out all the Flux books at
www.fluxnow.com

Leaving Paradise
SIMONE ELKELES

Nothing has been the same since Caleb Becker left a party drunk, got behind the wheel, and hit Maggie Armstrong. Even after months of painful physical therapy, Maggie walks with a limp. Her social life is nil and a scholarship to study abroad—her chance to escape everyone and their pitying stares—has been canceled.

After a year in juvenile jail, Caleb's free . . . if freedom means endless nagging from a transition coach and the prying eyes of the entire town. Coming home should feel good, but his family and ex-girlfriend seem like strangers.

Caleb and Maggie are outsiders, pigeon-holed as "criminal" and "freak." Then the truth emerges about what really happened the night of the accident and, once again, everything changes. It's a bleak and tortuous journey for Caleb and Maggie, yet they end up finding comfort and strength from a surprising source: each other.

ISBN: 978-0-7387-1018-1

5 ³⁄₁₆ x 8

264 pp. $8.95

Check out all the Flux books at
www.fluxnow.com

Hoops of Steel

John Foley

Basketball is Jackson O'Connell's life. Much more than a game, it allows him to cross barriers of class and race, and make new friends from the rival high school. Driven by his passion for hoops, he can almost forget his alcoholic father and a night of violence that tore his family apart.

Jackson's senior year is plagued by volcanic zits, girl shyness, and rumors that isolate him from most of the school. And when team politics keep him off the starting lineup of the basketball team, his hopes for a scholarship plummet like an airball. His self-confidence in tatters, Jackson makes errors on and off the court that almost cost him a friend and the girl of his dreams. With no rulebook to follow, Jackson must learn how to rebound from injustice and anger . . . and start shooting from the heart.

ISBN: 978-0-7387-0981-9

5 ³/₁₆ x 8

264 pp. $8.95

Check out all the Flux books at
www.fluxnow.com

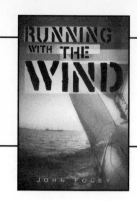

Running with the Wind
John Foley

Graduating from high school is supposed to feel like the beginning of your real life. But for Jackson O'Connell, it's more like a slew of endings. In this sequel to Hoops of Steel, Jackson's dream of a basketball scholarship is gone. His surrogate parent Granny Dwyer has died and he has no place to really call home. His relationship with Kelly is in crisis—Kelly is Princeton bound, while Jackson doesn't have a plan beyond the next five minutes. Even Jackson's alcoholic father seems to be getting his life together. Introduced to a gruff old sailor at Granny's funeral, Jackson reluctantly agrees to live at the marina and work at the boatyard. As Jackson experiences the rigors of working for a living and learning how to sail, he gains skills and self-knowledge. Is it enough to help him navigate the challenges he faces and set his own course for the future?

ISBN: 978-0-7387-1002-0
5 ³⁄₁₆ x 8
216 pp. $8.95

Check out all the Flux books at
www.fluxnow.com